GODS
OF THE NEW
MOONS

a novella

J.L. Forrest

inspired by music from

King Makis

NiceFM

"Re-Entry"

First Edition. Paperback. Published by the Robot Cowgirl Press:

http://robotcowgirl.com.

Design by Forstå.

Cover by Victor Laszlo.

Library of Congress Cataloging-in-Publication Data has been applied for.

ISBN 978-1-950552-99-3

FURTHER READING [AND LISTENING]

Read more of J.L. Forrest—
REQUIES DAWN (a novel of the far future)
DELICATE MINISTRATIONS (short fictions)
MINUSCULE TRUTHS (short fictions)

Songs at the End of the World—
WHEN THE WORLD ENDS
GODS OF THE NEW MOONS
QUEENS OF THE HORNED LORD (Coming 2019)
MEMORIES OF THE DAMNED (Coming 2019)
WHEN THE WORLD BEGINS (Coming 2019)

Join J.L. Forrest's Mailing List—
http://jlforrest.com/newsletter/

Visit J.L. Forrest's Website—
http://jlforrest.com

Listen to the Song for This Novella—
Hear "Re-Entry" by King Makis from NiceFM, and learn more about its creators at:

http://nicefm.bandcamp.com/track/re-entry

Thanks to—

King Makis

NiceFM

Johine

Marcus Aurelius Antoninus Augustus

and as always

Shana

I. A SINGLE PINE

2131.4.8.23:04 GMT
Alt 40.1E6m
High Earth Orbit
EIK-Cel Station

ROBOTS LOCK ME INTO a lozenge not much bigger than a coffin, and inside a pressure harness they clip the baby to my chest. Two technicians supervise the procedure before launching me, and the baby, into space.

Requiring no more force than a gentle nudge, the lozenge eases from the airlock at the same orbital velocity as EIK-Cel Station, and a weak thrust angles us into an approach. Relative to Earth's surface the baby and I are moving at 26,295 kilometers per hour, and we'll enter the atmosphere doing Mach 21.

I hold my tiny, precious passenger, caressing his grapefruit-sized head, enjoying the soft down of his dark hair, marveling at his calm. The lozenge ushers us smoothly toward the stratopause. Excepting minor lurches, the baby and I float, meshed to the lozenge's frame.

The baby's smell calms me.

I attribute this calming to evolutionary biology, one of nature's tricks, short-circuiting the self-preservation instincts of otherwise functionally selfish adults. Adults will commit suicide to save a baby. For months I've been one of this infant's caretakers, I know babies don't always smell good, and for now I'm confined with a helpless shit-making machine. While I can, I breathe another lungful of clean-baby scent.

My own laughter surprises me and, joining me, the baby coos. Air vibrates through his lips and his spittle floats free. In zero gravity, this spit gathers into a wobbling sphere, following the currents of our breaths. By some deeper command of physics, I know that spit will end up on me.

In front of my face, a fifteen-by-ten centimeter window frames the growing edge of Earth's atmosphere. Our acute approach will minimize friction *and* slow the lozenge on a long ride through the stratosphere and past the tropopause. As we near the frictional threshold, the lozenge rolls me, pointing my toes in our direction of travel. Facing *up*, I realize this is the first time I've ever used Earth as my relative center. I don't bother looking for Station, not in this light. Earth reflects too much sunlight, too bright for any stars, and Sol shines a few degrees outside my angle of vision.

Our deceleration begins as a faint tug toward my feet. For several minutes it's as if I'm standing inside the outer ring of Station, a perfect and comfortable *1g*, then strengthening forces distribute along my back like I'm reclining on a hillside.

Not bad, easier than expected, but my passenger looses a high-pitched shriek. He hiccups and screams more, and here's something the technicians never designed for—within confined, hard-shelled spaces, a baby's cries reach ear-splitting volumes.

The flight engineers had calculated well, meaning we never exceed *2.1g* and even that soon passes. The sky transitions from matte black to soft blue.

In the subsequent silence I fear the baby has died, that the minimal reentry forces proved too much for his small body. But no, he's sleeping again, peaceful as can be.

From the ground, anyone watching our arrival would have witnessed a bright arc. Yet on Earth few witnesses remain. My passenger and I will add two to their number—we are aliens here, first-timers, though I'm certain I know more about this world, factually, than do most of its residents.

The lozenge's comm sounds in my ear: "Your vitals are good, Aur. How you feeling?"

The voice belongs to Mr. Avidità. He rates this mission *critical,* has reiterated its risks.

"I'm feeling fantastic, Your Grace. Thank you."

"Good," he says. "We'll watch you all the way. Do confirm your health and position before scuttling the drop-craft."

"Yes, Your Grace."

He didn't need to remind me of my tasks or our protocols—I'm a Harque and we seldom forget. His words, I figure, are for his own benefit, a stress response. The King isn't allowed to show doubt, but he must sometimes feel it.

"Once you abandon the lozenge," he says, "the satellites will keep an eye on you as long as they can."

Flaps extend from the lozenge's exterior, the g-forces multiply, and again the baby squawks. The wind roars, too, resistance and fluctuations in air pressure shaking the airframe. Outside the window, clouds envelop us in a soft, hazy, white nothing.

The altimeter reads four kilometers. We'll hit the deck at about twelve hundred meters, three degrees from horizontal, and we're still clipping along at more than the speed of sound.

As we impact, the lozenge's AI will measure forces in three dimensions, and its frame-inside-a-frame construction will engage counter-forces to cushion the inertia. The slightest error, a delay of milliseconds, will reduce me and the baby to bonemeal and liquefied flesh inside an expensive can of carbon-ceramic titanium.

The sole life which a man can lose is that which he is living at the moment, wrote my namesake. *The longest life and the shortest amount to the same thing.*

The baby needs a diaper change. I'm grateful he waited this long.

The noise must terrify him, the cacophony as the shell deflects earth and stones. We bounce then hit again, yawing to starboard, and I'm afraid we'll roll. I grit my teeth but, slowly, the lozenge grinds to a stop.

Beyond my viewport, a single pine tree points back toward orbit, through a sky the color of eggplant, an evening shade. We've landed on that narrow line which I have ten thousand times observed from altitude, the threshold between Earth's night and its day, and I've arrived in time to experience my first terrestrial sunset.

No time, however, to admire it.

The baby calms again. His diaper change will have to wait until I can put some distance between us and our landing site, because anyone might have witnessed our fall from heaven.

And at these latitudes there're cannibals.

II. CHRISTMAS MORNING

Recollected
2111.12.25.10:17 GMT
Alt 40.2E6m
High Earth Orbit
EIK-Cel Station

IN MY COHORT I wasn't the smartest, but I wasn't an idiot either. By Christmas Day of my seventh year, I'd a sense of my value to Mr. Avidità. He afforded me more attention than he did the other boys, though this made them hate me.

My seven-year-old self, sitting in an exam chair in a room of polished titanium:

From the other side of a small table, Ms. Trotsky's smile encouraged me, and she held up her hand, alerting me to prepare. I sat straighter and focused.

"What sort of rock is limestone?" she asked.

"Sedimentary," I answered.

"What is its chemical composition?"

"Calcium carbonate, Miss."

"Marble is also calcium carbonate. Is it limestone?"

"No, Miss. Same composition, different sort of rock."

"What sort would that be?"

"Metamorphic."

"Can you name another natural form in which we might find calcium carbonate?"

"Stalactites and stalagmites."

"Good. Where did most of the calcium for limestone originate?"

"On seabeds."

"From what?"

"Prehistoric marine creatures."

The exam-room portal dilated and Mr. Avidità entered. He wore no tie, perhaps owing to the holiday, and his hands were in his pockets. Casual, relaxed, at ease. Observing from the doorway, he gestured for us to continue.

"Let's change the subject," said Ms. Trotsky. "The monarchs of England in order."

"Egbert," I said, then, "Aethelwulf, Aethelbald, Aethelberht, Aethelred, Alfred the Great—"

"What made him great?"

"He drove the vikings from the Isles and united England."

"Continue."

"Aethelstan, Edmund, Eadred, Eadwig, Edgar, Edward the Martyr, Aethelred the Second, Sweyn Forkbeard, then Aethelred again, then Edmund the Second. Cnut, Harold the First, Harthacnut—"

Mr. Avidità cleared his throat. "Enough," he said. "I'm sure Aurelius knows the others, to the last?"

"Queen Victoria the Second."

"How's young Aurelius doing, Ms. Trotsky?"

"A smart and sensitive boy," she said.

Mr. Avidità nodded. "His recall scores?"

"Ninety-ninth percentile, sir."

"Creative and improvisational?"

"High middle."

"Empathy?"

"Also high middle, sir."

He narrowed his eyes, seeming to consider my *empathy*. "Languages?"

"Eighty-ninth percentile."

"Mathematics and logic?"

"Ninety-second percentile, sir."

"Admirable." He smiled at me, and I loved his smile. All the boys did. The King of EIK-Cel, of all the Avidità Stations. The paterfamilias. Our father. "You've been patient this morning, Aur."

I faced him, still in my chair.

"It's Christmas," he said, offering his hand to me, and I leapt from my seat to put my hand in his. "We've had enough schooling for the morning. You too, Ms. Trotsky, you can power yourself down, presuming you've no further functions to complete."

She stood, her smile reserved, her hands clasped. "Very good, sir." At the corner of the room, she settled into an antique chair behind an old wooden desk, her posture perfect. Her eyes closed and she stilled.

The portal beside Mr. Avidità opened. "Come along, Aur."

"Where're we going?" I asked.

"I'd like to administer one more test today. That okay with you, Aur?"

I admit I hesitated, held by something in Mr. Avidità's tone, something which I've since recognized as signifying his natural showmanship. For every mystery he divulges, he holds a hundred others in reserve.

At last I said, "It's all right, Your Grace," because what else would I say? I was seven and he was the King.

He led me from the sleeping Ms. Trotsky, and we entered a long hallway which admitted sunshine from Station's high inner edge.

Mr. Avidità guided me down a breezeway between my school building and the crèche dormitories. Beautiful buildings, reminiscent of medieval Japanese fortresses but fashioned of ornately printed carbons, titaniums, and teakwood. He led me downstairs into a cherry-blossom garden, then below ground— into the tube's service corridors and finally to an airlock.

Pure diamondide, the lock's inner and outer doors allowed me an unobstructed view into space. Here the centripetal gravity exceeded *1g*, though only by a few percent. On the floor, inside the airlock, a gray rabbit stood on a square of lawn framed in aluminum.

My heart raced.

"I'm giving you a choice, Aurelius." Mr. Avidità squeezed my hand, reassuring me. "Either option is acceptable— no wrong answers."

I looked up at him.

"First option," he said. "You can have anything you want, anything in my power to give you."

"Can you give me my mother, Your Grace?"

"That I *cannot* do, Aurelius. You weren't born of a woman." He chuckled and shook his head. "Still, I'm the wealthiest man in System—you could be my heir?"

The rabbit's nose twitched, its long ears rotating. It nibbled the grass.

"Second option," said Mr. Avidità. "You can have this bunny. Love it, nurture it, give it as long and comfortable a life as you can."

Shaking its head, the rabbit hopped onto the airlock's cold floor, decided it didn't like the cold, then jumped back to the grass for more munches.

"What if I *do* want to be your heir?" I asked.

Mr. Avidità pointed to the wall beside us. On it, a panel displayed many controls. Two old-fashioned mechanical switches, buttons really, occupied its center. One red and one green.

"Hit the red button, Aurelius," said Mr. Avidità, "and you'll launch the bunny into space. This afternoon, I'll sign the documents declaring you my heir."

The bunny's eyes, a soft brownish-blue hazel unknown in humans, searched for the next succulent blades of grass. I observed in those eyes such innocence and vulnerability. I was a runty child, smaller than my more aggressive peers, but the rabbit was smaller still.

Laying his hand on my shoulder, Mr. Avidità said, "What would you like for your Christmas present, Aurelius?"

I hit the green button.

III. MY LATEST MURDERS

2131.4.8.19:44 PST
58°56'05.0"N 130°47'00.6"W
Alt 1,113m
British Columbia (Dissolved)
Stikine Region
224km to Destination

I WAITED TOO LONG before detonating the lozenge. Disappointing to have begun with an error, to have already taken lives. A loss of life, I have always felt, points to some earlier and more essential error and I told myself, before departing EIK-Cel Station, I'd try to get this done without killing.

With two exceptions.

Maybe.

I'm jogging now. My headlamp glows red, revealing only enough terrain to choose my route. I have trained for this, my paces smooth and steady, no great discomfort to my passenger. My goal is to put ten more kilometers between us and the wildfire which grows behind us.

After sunset the Milky Way embraces the horizons, an endless stream, and from where I'm standing it might *be* the milk of a Goddess—divine Hera breastfeeding the infant Heracles, her milk washing the firmament. Tempting, this romance, but the only Gods which have ever existed are New.

I should have ignited the lozenge *before* changing the baby's diaper.

My headlamp is a simple unidirectional LED. Everything I'm carrying is low tech by Avidità standards—nothing which a backpacker couldn't have scrounged from REI before the collapse of the global economies, nothing I can't explain away to anyone I encounter. My 105-liter backpack holds fifty-three compact diapers, baby paraphernalia, ample wipes, a carbon-fiber tent, a lightweight sleeping bag, an insulated pad, a camp stove, fifteen kilos of dried food, first-aid and emergency kits, overland gear, binoculars, a change of clothes, blankets, a three-liter water bladder, a water filter, flares, ammunition, a dozen sealed feeding bottles, and sixteen kilos of formula—brands still produced in North American until Blight. At my hip I carry a mint fifty-five-year-old Walther P99 AS with a fifteen-round magazine.

The lozenge brought us down within a wide, scalloped valley, terrain carved during the last ice age. In the minutes before sunset, I climbed a boulder and surveyed the stunted pines dotting the valley from the edge of the Eastern Mountain Plateau to the foothills of the Boundary Ranges. In these valleys many trees are dead, but more still live, and many appear young. A black line of burnt foliage crosses several kilometers northeast, but to my eye the burn looks old. To my nose, which has never known an atmosphere outside the Stations, terraria, and interplanetary vessels, the air reeks of woodsmoke.

Many wildfires still ravage this world, most around the equator and in Russia.

Our landing had to have been spectacular—this slender black bullet screaming in at three hundred kilometers an hour, flaps open, parachute deployed. We plowed a kilometer-long trench through a marshland, splashing mud and grass all the way.

In thirty-seven seconds I'd cleared the lozenge, backpack in place, baby in his harness, and I sprinted five hundred meters west before ducking behind a granite outcropping. The baby hiccoughed and whimpered but, to my relief, held back the full force of his lungs. I afforded six minutes to observe the abandoned lozenge, its cockpit open wide, and also the surrounding area.

Peaceful. The evening downslopes whispered from the hillsides.

I laid down the backpack, retrieved a diaper, and got to work. Off came the old diaper, wrapped and taped, and this I buried. I wiped him clean, laughed with him, played peekaboo, and—

Voices on the wind.

I peered over the outcropping. Two men and a woman investigated the lozenge. Nearby, four old-fashioned, electric-powered ATVs awaited, parked and powered down. An ATV *would* be convenient. I wouldn't have to lug a forty-four-kilo pack, I wouldn't have to jog, and we might make better time.

But I'd have to fight for one and I didn't like those odds.

From my pocket I eased the lozenge's self-destruct switch and, before tossing it away, I triggered it.

The drop vessel exploded, an oxygen-fed burst of powdered magnesium which for seven seconds burned at 2200°C. Not in a roar, but like a dragon taking a breath, this consumed everything around it. The ATVs melted to rims and frame, and nothing but bones remained of their riders. That pine which had first greeted me glowed a magnificent orange, a candle flame to heaven, instantly gone.

I finished changing the diaper.

"Hey, motherfucker," the man said.

He stood behind me, holding a rifle, not braced against his shoulder but slung low like an electric guitar. He blinked in shock, his jaw hanging, overcome at how his friends or family or whoever they'd been had died. His clothes were threadbare, one of his flannel-shirt buttons missing. A month's worth of beard covered his face.

"You killed them," he said, raising his gun.

The baby squealed, drawing his attention.

I shot him between the eyes. *Not* how I wanted this to begin.

Now I figure I'm three klicks west of my latest murders. I don't feel good about them, but I don't feel bad either. I wipe my sweaty palms on my jacket, and one comes back smeared with baby drool—that wobbling sphere I'd noted on the way down from orbit.

I'm at a full-on run and the baby's closed his eyes again.

IV. NEW YEAR'S DAY

Recollected
2112.1.1.8:44 GMT
Alt 40.1E6m
High Earth Orbit
EIK-Cel Station

I NAMED THE RABBIT Flapjacks. Why isn't important.

On Christmas morning, the other children played in the dormitory's great room or in the cherry-blossom garden. They banged around with new toys they could've printed themselves, but these toys had arrived in wrapping paper and therefore generated real excitement. I carried Flapjacks with me to the design lab, where I managed to cobble together plans for a hutch. While printshop drones completed the hutch, I read everything I could about the history and safe-keeping of rabbits.

Seven days after adopting him, on New Year's Day, I sat in a comfortable chair in a quiet reading room in the dormitory's upper levels. Flapjacks rested in my lap, accepting a good petting, digesting a carrot.

Sunlight streamed through the windows, and Earth rotated into view. Mr. Avidità paid me a visit, not in person this time, but projected by drone.

"How's Flapjacks?" he asked.

"Doing well, Your Grace."

"You made an excellent choice, Aurelius."

I stroked Flapjacks between the ears. Through the windows, South America swept into view, and Earth occupied eigh-

teen degrees of my vision. I'd been studying the Amazon rain-
forests, often by telescope. When I first began observing them,
I noted how anemic and sparse they appeared compared to the
satellite imagery in the records. During the months of my
study, they shrank. Swathes of tan and dark brown. Daily the
river's dirty waters thinned and, while giant Pacific storms
dropped incredible rains into the watersheds, the runoff carried
more topsoil and clay into the Atlantic.

"Earth is dying," I said, "isn't it?"

Mr. Avidità frowned, slipping his virtual hands into his
virtual pockets. "That remains to be seen. The old girl *has*
taken a beating."

"We all came from Earth."

"*Humanity* came from Earth," he said, "though *you* were
born here on EIK-Cel."

"From an artificial womb." I hadn't meant my words to
carry so much self-loathing, so much disappointment.

"You and your crèche-mates are *miracles,* Aurelius.
Never think otherwise. The advances which allow *you* to
exist, we're using them to resurrect ten thousand extinct
species. The innovations in mining and extraction which
caused so much pollution down *there,*" he said, meaning
Earth, "have allowed us to core nickel-iron asteroids and build
terraria where elephants roam savannas without fear of poachers,
where wolves hunt a tundra without the terror or rifles and
snares. What *you* are, Aurelius, is a culmination of all Creation.
Be proud."

Sniffling, I nodded. "Yes, Your Grace."

"Happy New Year, Aur."

"Happy New Year, Your Grace."

"There's no school today. Go enjoy yourself."

His hologram vanished and the drone which had projected it flew away. I returned Flapjacks to his hutch, changed his water, and gave him a fresh bowl of pellets and lettuce. That afternoon I did a lot of playing outside—*outside* meaning something different to a boy who grew up on Station rather than Earth—and I remember each detail, each taste of pollen, the scent of grass smeared into the knees of my pants.

Before the end of the day, one of the other boys punched me in the nose, and to this day the flavor of that blood at the back of my throat remains distinct. They teased me relentlessly. I, the one who cared for animals, who felt fear, who in my early years suffered night terrors and wet myself.

Oh, yes, they beat me.

In the crèches, Mr. Avidità allowed a certain amount of violence, and I accepted that. Wishing for an existence without violence seemed as stupid as wishing for a world with unicorns.

My namesake once wrote, *Is one doing me wrong? Let himself look to that; his actions are his own.*

Our cosmos is brutish, which was clear enough to me at that guiltless age. Why should the existence of brutes ever surprise anyone?

V. STAKED VICTIMS

2131.4.9.10:37 PST
58°47'10.5"N 132°07'19.6"W
Alt 277m
British Columbia (Dissolved)
Stikine Region
146km to Destination

IN STRENGTH AND AGGRESSION I never matched the other boys, even into our teens and twenties. Those alphas now command military units against the Nesteler Group or the UPRC, but they can have that life. I don't want it.

Yet I can run as fast as any of those assholes and twice as gracefully. I can glide.

Since detonating the lozenge, I've covered sixty-five kilometers, stopping last night for six hours, during which I and the baby slept. While I'm fresh I'm pushing hard, before I reach the foothills and Boundary Ranges. It'll be slower going there, though routes exist today which were closed before the world grew warmer.

By morning, clouds blanket the sky. I'm unaccustomed to them, as I am to a horizon which drops forever from me as I follow the watershed. It drains toward the Alaskan Panhandle, gathering all the moisture the Pacific can throw at it, and the misty mountains rise around me. The Inklin River Valley bursts with greenery, so many species their names exceed Ms. Trotsky's best efforts to teach me botany.

Not that I failed to memorize each plant I studied—a Harque seldom forgets—but many of these species do not appear in Station's records, and the satellite images suggested fewer trees, especially on the region's south-facing slopes, than grow around me now.

Cedar, hemlock, orchids, mushrooms, worts, and endless varieties of fern—much of this vegetation should no longer survive, climate has shifted so much and so suddenly, and around the world the fires burn and floods wash nutrients into the bleached seas.

Here, life blooms.

Perhaps I simply lack perspective, having never seen it in person before?

Sometimes the baby cries to be fed, to be changed, to crawl, or to lie still. His complaints, however, seldom last long. He babbles and wiggles like any three-month old, like any of the other younglings in the crèches. I suspect he's no more human-standard than I, and while he cries and drools like most babies, sometimes his focus sharpens and his gaze dissects everything before it.

An adult gaze.

Then he naps again or needs a new diaper. Only a baby after all.

By midday the clouds disperse and Sol warms the air into a soup. My sweat gathers into cascades, gluing the backpack to my spine, bunching my pants between my thighs. Pills balance my sodium and provide electrolytes, I stop jogging long enough to heat food for me and formula for the baby, and I hurry on.

I parallel the riverbank, and the Inklin channels me between the tree line and endless marshes. Insects swarm and hum. The river tends north and eventually it will join another tributary, bearing southwest toward New Juneau.

Clouds come and go, but when the sun shines, it shines unforgivingly. Though I place a mesh sunscreen over the baby, keeping it there through the afternoon, I worry he might sunburn.

By five o'clock I've covered another fourteen klicks and, for the first time since scuttling the lozenge, I need a good rest. I hike into the trees and they shade us, giving me a place to sit, cook dinner, and check the diaper. The baby cries, hungry, but I feed him as Sol dips behind the hills. Laying out a blanket for him, I let him crawl.

Maybe there's time for me to eat in peace.

From downriver a moan catches my ear, deep enough to be a man's. I sit still, not chewing, scarcely breathing. The moan rises, piteous, and I leave my meal unfinished. After packing, I strap the baby to my chest, babbling nonsense at him, distracting him, calming him.

Bushwhacking through scrub and ferns, I cut westward without leaving the forest. Beyond a crest opens an unfamiliar stretch of the river which bows through wild grasses. At this meadow's heart stand five tall poles, squarely erect.

No, not poles, but *stakes*. Vlad Dracula, I've read, once impaled twenty-thousand men in a single day. By comparison, I suppose, what I'm looking at seems mild.

Three men and two women, all naked, each penetrated in the same horrific place. Blood crosses paint their chests. For each, the stake exited differently—through the neck, from the arched back, beside the shoulder—and only one man still lives. He grips the top of his stake as if he might keep himself from sliding lower, as if he might lift himself off it and save his life.

I tug the sunscreen over the baby's face while my right hand falls to the handle of my pistol. Studying the meadow, the river, and the trees, assuring myself no one else watches, I take three steps into the open.

Spotting me, the dying man's eyes widen. Two more steps, and I stand so close he could spit on me. Nailed to one stake is a wooden sign, but the wrong side faces me, and I've no idea what's on it.

"Who did this?" I ask him.

"The Horned Lords," he replies.

"Why?"

"Because we're Christians."

I want to turn away, to vomit, but I hold my ground. "They stake Christians, do they?"

"Staked *us.*" He wheezes.

"What did you do? To make them do this to you?"

Blood flecks his lips. "Nothing."

I wait, wondering if he'll offer something more helpful, wondering if he'll die first. In the silence, the chirping of crickets fills the meadow. The river burbles. The baby jabbers.

"We were," he says, gasping between words, "trying to cross the Bonlin."

"What's the Bonlin?"

"*The Bone Line.*" He coughs. More blood. "Trying to bring the Good News to New Juneau."

I still don't understand, but I ask, "No luck, huh?"

"This is Satan's land. They call him *Nodens,* but we know his true name—" His words fade, a man out of breath, out of time.

"That stake missed your heart," I say, "but you're not going to live long."

"Praise Jesus," he says.

The baby coos, kicks, wobbles.

"What do you know about the Queens of the Horned Lord?" I ask.

He laughs, coughs, spits a bubble of blood from between his teeth. *"I will shew unto thee the judgment of the great whore that sitteth upon many waters*—only there're two!"

A quote from the *King James,* though I'm not much for the Testaments, Old or New.

"Any last requests?" I ask.

"Say a prayer for us."

"May the Lord bless you and keep you." I draw the Walther and fire.

The report echoes across the valley. All the fight and tension leave the man's body, his arm no longer braced against the stake, and he slides another meter toward the ground. Fresh blood coats the wood, dark in the fading daylight. I walk to the other side of the sign.

THE OLD GODS RULE HERE

Holstering the gun, I jog west. Sol edges toward the hilltops, and I'm wishing now for a pair of Avidità Corporation multivision goggles or ocular implants. But no, Mr. Avidità wanted me low-fi for this mission. Strict orders. When it grows too dark, I switch on my headlamp.

I'd hoped to camp around here this evening, to enjoy some solid rest. Less than fifteen minutes since I pulled that trigger, and I've covered another klick, west once more.

The baby's gone back to sleep. At least there's that.

VI. GODS OF THE NEW MOONS

Recollected
2116.5.18.14:57 GMT
Alt 40.1E6m
High Earth Orbit
EIK-Cel Station

F LAPJACKS FLOURISHED.
Such a sweet disposition, that rabbit, and after study hours also a frequent companion. I liked him more than I liked most people, and I played with him, cared for him, and often brought him fresh greens and vegetables.

I became the boy with the bunny.

This sometimes led to beatings, but the boys never touched the rabbit. They knew whose gift he'd been.

One day, Mr. Avidità invited me for breakfast. This required me to leave the crèche and travel several Sectors of Station, past four residential discuses and several farms.

To imagine Station is, I've come to understand, difficult for those who've never experienced it. The ring-torus's outer diameter measures ten kilometers, while its inner spans 7.85. Carbon-composite cross-spokes strengthen its circumference, unconnected to any hub but interlaced in cords. This creates a tough-yet-pliable, airtight, double-shelled inner tube with a volume of eighty-eight cubic kilometers. At 222 meters per second per second, its centripetal acceleration grants a perfect *1g* to its inner curve. To either side of that tube, as the curves approach vertical, grow terraced fields and farms, and above those hang hydroponic facilities, suspended in tension from the torus's so-called roof. Through this meters-thick shell, windows of diamondide offer views into space.

More than thirty-one kilometers of ribbon city fill the *1g* circumference, including residential discuses only sixty meters across but nearly a kilometer high—an extraterrestrial urban plan which could have been drawn by Le Corbusier. Up to a hundred thousand people live in each discus, a million inhabitants in Station. These dense vertical towns nestle with atmospherically attenuated microbiomes, the largest botanical gardens humanity has ever known. Not many animals in Station—Avidità Corporation maintains terraria for those—but Station grows vegetation aplenty, along with pollinators natural and artificial.

Mr. Avidità's multistory home occupies the middle of an agricultural Sector, surrounded by hectares of rice paddies.

His guardians, Apollo and Ares, escorted me from the house's front doors to the high veranda which overlooked the King's private gardens. Leaving me, the two AIs skulked away on all fours in the canine-like, composite bodies they most often occupied. The gardens exhibited plants from across Earth, many extinct in their native ranges, but Mr. Avidità made no attempt to curate these with any regional precision. He, his gardeners, or his AIs made each choice for their aesthetics, fashioning hectares of pleasure gardens with riots of color and perfume, hanging gardens and lily ponds, meditative grottoes, edible gardens, shaded gardens for strolling, sunny gardens for promenading, gardens for dinner parties, resting gardens and wrestling gardens, endless flower gardens, and an olive orchard.

At the veranda's center, Mr. Avidità stood from a small breakfast table, gesturing to the chair across from him. I sat awkwardly, a taller boy by then but also lanky. He returned to his seat and poured apple juice into our glasses.

"Welcome, Aurelius."

"Thank you, Your Grace."

"How's Flapjacks?"

"Well. He hops, eats, poops. He's a good rabbit."

Four servers set the breakfast, bringing eggs, sautéed vegetables, toast, milk, butter, jam, and tea. Without another word, as if the father and son of some ordinary family, Mr. Avidità and I filled our plates and tucked in.

"The gardens *are* lovely today," he said, "aren't they?"

"So many flowers in bloom."

"We modeled the grounds after the Villa Adriana."

Swallowing a bite of eggs, I looked over the green, past cypresses whose high crowns didn't quite reach our balcony.

He nodded, speaking between bites. "Today most *all* of Roma is ruins, fewer humans living there than during the Gothic Wars or after its sacking by Charles the Fifth."

"Was Villa Adriana so—"

"Ostentatious?"

"I was going to say *lush,* Your Grace." I took my tea black.

Nodding, he poured milk into his. "How's your breakfast?"

"Delicious!"

Servants whisked empty plates from the table, refilled drinks, and scraped away crumbs. A young woman leaned across the table, balanced on her toes. I studied her, wondering if Mr. Avidità had hired her from among the refugees, if he'd grown her, or if his engineers had finally developed androids which bridged the uncanny valley.

That had been Nesteler's corporate niche for some time.

The tip of the woman's tongue squirreled from the corner of her mouth, and a tightening at the edge of her eye suggested stress. A worry, perhaps, that she'd underperform in front of the most powerful man in System. *Not* a robot then.

Probably not crèche-born either.

The last plates vanished, and for a while we drank tea and he asked about my studies, my enmities with the other crèche boys, my feelings about life aboard Station.

"I like it, Your Grace."

"Like?"

"It's home," I said.

"When I was growing up, my home was a hellhole." His smile remained fixed, more studied than spontaneous, and he stared long enough to make me shift in my seat. "Ever gone camping, Aur?"

I pressed my palms to the table edge. "What do you mean?" Station was *big*, but it had few places for *camping*.

"I need to visit one of the terraria, check its operations, see if I can outmaneuver a developing problem. Would you join me?"

Leave Station?

"Will there be animals, Your Grace?"

"Quite a few, yes." His smile grew.

"How far to the terraria?"

"On the arc I have planned? We'll do a six-hundred-fifty-million-klick round trip."

"How long will it take?" Beyond Earth's orbit, I didn't know much then about the corporation's activities, could make only educated guesses about its technologies.

"A month?" he said. "Not much longer, or we'll lose the return window."

My heart thumped. Of course I'd go, and he knew it before he'd asked.

He gestured, triggering the room's AI. The windows darkened and holographic projections filled the air above the table: a model of System, including Sol, the planets to Saturn, the Asteroid Belt, major moons, and G- and C-class artificial objects. Out of scale, of course, but legible and elegantly designed, conveying abstract information, not distance.

"Orwellian Theory," he said, "argues any great struggle always shakes out to three tyrannical powers, no more and no less."

Faint primary colors overlaid the hologram, punctuated by bright points.

"The colors," he said, "represent the territories of the UPRC, Nesteler Group, and Avidità Corporation. The points are important nexuses, extraterrestrial cities, stations, or artificial moons."

"The Gods of the New Moons," I said, though to this day I'm not sure why I said it.

Mr. Avidità blinked at me. "What was that, Aur?"

"There must be hundreds of stations and extraterrestrial cities now, aren't there?"

"More than a thousand."

"I've read the myths of the Greeks, Your Grace. The Egyptians, Norse, Chinese, Japanese, and others too. The way they spoke about the Gods, Bifrost Bridges and Celestial Realms. Those were just stories, but what you and Nesteler and the UPRC have done—you *are* the Gods of New Moons, don't you think?"

"Poetic, Aur." His brief smile was indulgent, as if for a child.

Poetic? At the time I didn't know.

He continued, "We *Gods,* as you say, don't control equal territories, but we *do* possess nearly identical resources, in terms of raw materials, military assets, and sheer wealth. Each has stated a desire to save Earth, though we disagree on methods and I believe Nesteler would gleefully strip humanity's cradle to the proverbial bone."

"Why're you sharing this with me?"

The model planets orbited their artificial sun. "Because you're smarter than the other boys, Aur."

I never felt this way about myself. "I wish you'd tell *them* that."

"Why?"

"They hit me a lot."

"They hit you because they can *sense* there's something better about you, even if they can't pinpoint it."

"They're stronger than I am, they've got better reflexes, and their cognitive scores aren't *that* much lower."

He chuckled. "In the realms of excellence, Aur, fractional differences can mean glory or annihilation."

I nodded.

"I haven't interceded on their bullying," he said, "because I wanted to see how you'd take it."

My brows knit, though as I became conscious of this I relaxed, veiling my distress. "How have I *taken it?*"

"Stoically."

My namesake once wrote:

Be content with what you are, and wish not change; nor dread your last day, nor long for it.

Though I would've preferred *not* being punched, *not* being teased, *not* being bullied, what did it matter? It changed nothing about who I was or am. Nor was it, or has it, ever been worth writing my memories of those events, not even to inscribe the names of my persecutors. When I die, those meaningless memories will die with me.

"I'll say this about your physical scores," said Mr. Avidità, "you're the best cross-country runner I've ever known, one of the best who's ever lived."

This earned a true and delighted smile from me. "Thank you."

"We'll leave in three weeks, Aur. I'll show you lions and elephants."

Some of the best news I'd ever heard.

"Now, let's walk those gardens, shall we? The lilies are blooming."

VII. STRAGGLERS

2131.4.9.19:52 PST
58°46'20.2"N 132°32'44.1"W
Alt 171m
British Columbia (Dissolved)
Stikine Region
123km to Destination

WITH EACH KLICK SINCE leaving those five piteous Christians, I've imagined more malice in the darkness. For now I follow the swiftest route to New Juneau, though anyone journeying inland would cross my path, perhaps the sorts who impale the unwanted.

I do not believe in *Old Gods,* but I do believe in men who might do terrible things in their names.

If I abandon the valleys I can orienteer along higher ground to the coast, though the Ranges' lowest passes reach almost three thousand meters. Shorter distance to New Juneau but thrice the time, maybe more, maybe a lot more. I've memorized the topographical maps, but the differences between map and territory can mean the difference between life and death. Snow tops the peaks and deadfalls are too numerous to chance.

Besides, I don't have the food for an alpine journey, I definitely don't have the *formula,* and an encounter with the Horned Lords is inevitable anyway.

Necessary, in fact.

The skies remain clear but the air becomes chillier. Though I've stopped several times, the baby is now crying loud and long, and so I climb an escarpment, raise the tent, and seal us inside. To my relief he soon sleeps, fed and burped, and I bury his latest diaper as far away as I'm willing to risk walking in the dark on a steep hillside.

The air gets colder, maybe an incoming springtime storm. Maybe not, since the sky remains clear. The iridescent Milky Way glints and a frosty breeze shudders down the mountainsides, rattling the trees.

"Real slow," comes the raspy voice, "hold your arms out to your sides."

He's behind me, five or six paces. No clue whether he holds a weapon, so I obey.

"Pinch the butt of your pistol, unholster it, and toss it."

I do.

"Turn around."

The dim red of my headlamp reveals *two* men. The big one aims a carbine at me. The smaller man, gaunt and furtive, hunkers behind the larger. Animal furs drape them, like those of trappers or mountain men in bygone centuries.

"Maybe we can talk?" I suggest.

"Hush," says the bigger, then he whispers to the smaller.

"My name is Aurelius. You can call me Aur."

"Kneel," the bigger says to me, and I do. "Get down, face down. Cross your ankles. Hands on the back of your head."

I do everything he commands, and all the while I listen for the baby. Not a peep. The cedars, hawthorns, oaks, and pines creak in the wind. The smaller man takes my holster and the two extra clips of ammunition at my belt, then returns to hiding behind his bigger companion.

That one says, "What you doing in these woods, Aur?"

My cheek rests against dry, alkali soil, bare earth freckled with grasses. The scent of flaked mica and the tang of fallen pine needles almost make me sneeze.

"Trying to survive," I say, "same as you, I expect."

"Where you heading?" he asks.

"New Juneau."

"Why?"

"I'm hoping to meet the Queens of the Horned Lord—"

The furtive, gaunt one giggles.

"Not many left coming this way," says the bigger one, "who *aren't* coming for the Queens." He grunts, a soft acknowledgment.

"That's me then," I say.

"That your tent over there?" he asks.

"Yes."

"What'll we find when we search it?"

I clench my teeth. This is what I wished to avoid, why I was willing to kill those poor people at the lozenge—I can risk no threat to the baby. I prepare to act, to take a bullet and keep fighting. These men don't know how fast I can move, how much I can take, how hard I can hit.

"My gear," I say, "and a baby."

"What'd you say?" the smaller man asks.

"A baby."

The wind snatches their next words. In my headlamp's rosy glow rests a fist-sized stone, perfect for throwing or crushing bone.

"What're you doing with a baby?" the bigger asks.

"Out near Dease Lake, off old highway thirty-seven, there was a woman making a go of it." The lie is rehearsed. "The cabin was well stocked, she had farmland, was getting ready for the spring planting. She had an older son too, a boy about fourteen, and the baby. They were kind enough to put me up a few nights, figured maybe I'd stick around to help with the sowing."

"Did *you* kill them? Stock up on what you needed?"

The smaller scoffs. "Why would he *kill* the momma and teenager but *keep* the baby?"

The bigger pauses. "I don't know."

"The answer is no," I say. "There were bandits, four ass-holes, came looking for trouble. The baby and I, after it was done, we were the only two left breathing. I buried the mother and the older boy behind the house."

Grunting once more, the bigger says, "A sad story."

As if on cue, the baby hiccoughs.

"What're you going to do with us?" I ask.

More whispers. A chorus of distant coyotes drifts into the mix, and some part of my mind registers this, processes surprise at there being *any* coyotes in these hills. All over the world, a lot of apex predators have vanished.

The baby's hiccoughs grow into cries.

"My name is Garth," says the bigger.

The smaller says, "I'm Fitzpatrick."

"Nice to meet you," I say.

"Our job," says Fitzpatrick, "is to track down stragglers like you, the last few coming in from the continent, and round you up."

The coyotes carry on, as does the baby, as does the wind.

"Then what?" I ask.

"See what the fuck you're about," says Garth, "send you packing if you don't belong, bring you through the Bonlin if you do."

Again that word—*Bonlin*.

I ask, "What's the Bonlin exactly?"
Another giggle from Fitzpatrick. "You'll see."
Garth adds, "It's a *helluva* thing."

VIII. LIONS & ELEPHANTS

Recollected
2116.6.22.7:20 GMT
2.3 AU from Sol
Inner Asteroid Belt
Nearing Africa IV

A N M-TYPE PLANETOID, Africa IV's diameter measured 109 kilometers across its egg-shaped short axis. Almost fifty years ago, Avidità Corporation captured and mined it.

For iron—to alloy with titanium, molybdenum, vanadium, aluminum.

For nickel—to alloy with iron and molybdenum, and for rechargeable and recyclable batteries.

Africa IV was the greatest haul of iron and nickel in history. From it Avidità recovered 1.6e15 tonnes of refined iron and nickel, or eight thousand times the quantity extracted from Earth during the *entire* twenty-first century.

Five weeks after my breakfast with Mr. Avidità, we approached Africa IV in the *Plato,* his interplanetary trimaran. The planetoid appeared first as a lonely gray dot in the ship's cockpit windows. To starboard, Jupiter shined a few degrees past the bow of Orion, the gas giant tiny in my field of vision but brighter than it shone from Earth. For two days, the *Plato* had decelerated in docking preparations, culminating in AI-directed maneuvers.

As Africa IV loomed in our ports, its bigness awed me, as well as its artificialities. While most of its surface remained natural, rock and dark metals, one could not miss the polished arrays of its Solar bowl, its albedo near 1.0, pointing at Sol and refracting light into the planetoid's interior. Various artificial structures occupied the crust, some a hundred meters high and hundreds wide.

"It's an impressive facility," said Mr. Avidità, "isn't it?"

Certainly *vast*.

We drifted toward a structure which twinkled with electric lights. The AIs placed us in a synchronous spin, matching the planetoid's rotation, so we seemed to hover above one dock. This took time—Africa IV's surface rotated a kilometer per second—and our accelerating forces shifted gradually, slowly, almost imperceptibly from sideways to a sense of *up*, relative to Africa IV's axis. The *Plato* spun on all three axes, nose pointing away from Africa IV.

"You'll like what we've been doing here," Mr. Avidità said to me.

I knew what to expect, through reading or from holovids. I also couldn't *believe* it, not really. Though I did not so much as wiggle in my seat, I struggled to contain my excitement.

We docked, climbed from the *Plato,* and entered an airlock. Protocol brought us into a clean, orderly, oversized processing facility which required even Mr. Avidità to strip and submit to decontamination showers. We left our possessions in lockers and donned button-up linen shirts, heavy cotton slacks, cross-country boots, and broad hats. Past the changing-room doors, a young woman greeted us.

I never believed much in love at first sight, but *holy shit.*

She bowed, formal and graceful. Her complementary wilderness clothing would have been practical either for roughing it or for corporate picnics.

"Welcome to Africa Four, Mr. Avidità." She bowed again, to me, and I found myself returning the gesture. "Mr. Aurelius."

I had and have no last name.

Rising from her bow, she offered her hand and I shook it. "I'm Imka. I oversee Africa Four's predator populations."

I gawked. She didn't seem old enough for that job.

"If you'll follow me?" she said.

Her titian hair doubled as her halo, arcing across the top of her back and around her head. Her hips swayed, casting spells on me, on my almost-thirteen-year-old self, and I followed her like a puppy might trail an owner.

Behind us, two robots emerged from protective housings within an alloyed wall. Anodized in dark reds, they resembled jackals, loping elegantly on tall, slender, powerful legs. Their long snouts narrowed to points, and their tails swished.

"Come along, Apollo," said Mr. Avidità, waving for the AIs to follow. "Come along, Ares."

He, Imka, and I boarded an overland transport, which the AIs paced deftly, and Imka drove us through a five-hundred-meter-long spiraling passage, square in cross-section, aligning us with the centripetal rotation of Africa IV's interior. At the tunnel's end a blast door opened, and dazzling daylight burst over us, as bright as any I'd ever experienced aboard Station.

We were then as far from Earth as the Earth is from Sol.

The Savannah expanded before us as if, rather than traveling through space, we had traveled through time and found ourselves not in Africa IV but in Africa I, perhaps in Kenya, perhaps in the nineteenth century. Golden grasses and brush thrived in every direction and, behind me, much the same scene appeared, as the tunnel had spit us from a hillside. Punctuating the land, acacias stood as lone sentinels, casting deep shadows on the reddish earth. A palpable heat enveloped us.

Alongside us thundered a herd of wildebeests. Zebras accompanied them, and farther off wandered a tower of giraffes—a giant male, six females, and two calves. An odor of vegetation, dung, and dander infused the air, strong but not unpleasant.

"You might want to close your mouth," said Mr. Avidità, chuckling at me, "before it fills with flies."

The land drew my gaze farther still, and the horizon swept upward, a view I understood from a lifetime in Station, but here the scale exceeded reason. Clouds rolled through this volume, layered weather systems. As my focus shifted ever higher, I squinted, shaded my eyes, then closed them. Above us, the so-called sky shone piercingly bright.

As Avidità Corporation had mined Africa IV, the company reinforced its outer surface, leaving thick walls of composites, iron, and nickel. As it built the terrarium's atmosphere, bringing oxygen, nitrogen, argon, and trace gases from around System, it also nudged the planetoid's major axis into alignment with Sol. By then, engineers completed the arrays which reflected light from the terrarium's axis, a superstructure generating an artificial sun, "rising" every day in the "east" and "setting" each day in the "west."

Mr. Avidità's chuckle became a full-throated laugh, more genuinely happy than I'd ever heard him. "Breathtaking, isn't it?"

We rode the rest of the day in our transport, Imka at the controls, the AIs flanking us in their jackal bodies. At a watering hole, a parade of elephants trumpeted, bathed, and rolled in the mud, a calf playing amongst their legs. A wide river meandered through this land, its banks thick with reeds and rushes. I spotted a crocodile in a pool of gigantic lily pads.

In the west the reflecting array contracted, fading through yellows, oranges, and violets, and the land darkened. As it did, a moonlike glow appeared halfway down the axis, silvery white, creeping along the terrarium's spine.

Night fell. As if by magic, "stars" freckled the sky, roaming the axis in the millions, more like fireflies than distant, burning spheres of gas.

As our quiet-running vehicle neared the blast-door entrance from which we'd first emerged, the cackle of hyenas reached my ears, and Imka eased on the brakes.

Ahead of us, in the faint light, strolled a leisurely pride of lions. Two lionesses gazed at us, their jaws half open, their lower fangs bared. Afraid of nothing.

"Let's get back to the staff quarters," said Mr. Avidità.

"Yes, sir," replied Imka.

"I'm famished. How're you, Aur?"

I hadn't thought about food all day, couldn't now, could think only of the lions as they slunk into the shadows between the tall, dry grasses. "Hungry, yeah."

Back "underground," in facilities of steel, aluminum, titanium, and carbon, we gathered with three-dozen personnel. Their number included veterinarians, biologists, ecologists, engineers, doctors, scientists, and programmers. In a dining room we sat around a long wooden table, and a cook named Fred brought pots and platters of food.

We feasted.

"You're to be commended," Mr. Avidità told the team, applauding. "The data look excellent, populations are managed, bacteria and fungal growths measure well within norms, energy usages register optimal, waste management is doing as well as in any of the Stations. I'm proud of you."

Many thanked him. Sighs and laughter and smiles—their relief and joy were tangible.

"But we have a problem," he said, "which is why I'm here."

They waited, bracing themselves.

"We've intercepted communiques from Nesteler Group," he said. "Nesteler has learned of this facility, and they mean to target it."

Shocked whispers passed around the table. Expressions faded from triumph to terror.

"They would take it from us," he said, "or destroy it."

One woman covered her mouth.

"We operate on redundancy here," he said, "so I can evacuate half of you. You'll take a shuttle Earthward and, if everything turns out fine, we'll rotate you right back. The rest of you are too critical, this facility too sensitive, and you'll have to remain. As you know, we've automated ninety-nine-point-nine percent of everything which happens here but, more than elsewhere, we need your human eyes working alongside the AIs."

One woman nodded. "We understand, sir."

Her gray hair marked her as older than the others. I admired her bearing, the clarity of her expression. The terrarium's commander, I figured.

"I'll help sort the stayers and the goers," she said.

"Thank you, Tilda."

"What happens now?" asked the cook.

"I brought military assets with me," Mr. Avidità said. "In fact I deployed them on arrival."

During our flight I'd spotted none, but that didn't mean they weren't there. Always, Mr. Avidità kept his secrets.

He continued, "Unfortunately our nearest Dreadnaught, the *Alstad,* will be some hours getting here. In the meantime I'm doing everything I can to keep you safe."

Tilda inclined her head. "Thank you, sir."

I watched Mr. Avidità's face, read in it a practiced weariness, a mastered gravitas. "I can't guarantee anything," he said, "though I'll answer any questions you have. First, though, what about dessert?"

IX. THRESHOLDS

2131.4.9.21:28 PST
58°45'57.2"N 132°37'14.4"W
Alt 219m
British Columbia (Dissolved)
Stikine Region
119km to Destination

I HOLD THE BABY while Fitzpatrick empties my pack and searches my gear. Garth stashes my pistol and ammunition in his satchel, and his loaded carbine either hangs from its sling or rests in his hands. Once Fitzpatrick completes the search, they let me reorganize my pack, the baby fidgeting under a blanket beside me, and I jam the tent into its bag.

Adjusting my headlamp, I get my first excellent look at them. Garth like a badger. Fitzpatrick like a weasel. With the manners of men doing a job, neither at ease nor unduly concerned, they divide their attention between me and the woodlands.

"The baby needs downtime," I say.

"Soon," says Garth. "Our journey won't be long."

Longer than I like, as it turns out. Three hours.

Half the time the baby sleeps, some of the time I get him to suckle a pacifier or my finger, and the rest of the time he cries. From one side of the valley to the other, anything could hear him.

The silvered moonlight and cloudless stars *hint* more than *light* the way, but Garth and Fitzpatrick march confidently, familiarly along a game trail. It widens, joins another trail, and converges into a true road, leveled and laid with gravel.

To either side of it the trees tower, giants, boughs vaulting the road. Pines array themselves like soldiers, like the cyclops Polyphemus and his hundred sons waiting to ambush us. The road empties into a clearing. Around it hunker several wooden buildings, their windows intact, their walls solid. Yet no candles or electric lights shine from the interiors.

A way-station it looks like, a customs house, a border control now abandoned and no longer needed. I imagine its story—for a few years, thousands upon thousands would have followed this route from the east. Then, thousands would have trickled to dozens, and now to me. The world has emptied, populations committed to solitary and tribal lives, gathered into new centers, flown to space, or dead. Now the way-station waits to rot. The scent of livestock irritates my nose, piles of drying manure and hitching posts nearby, but no animals are here. The river murmurs through walls of vegetation, and ahead a bridge crosses a narrow, rushing tributary. Past it the road extends into shadow.

Poles decorate the clearing's center, reminding me of the stakes upon which the Christians died. In the dozens, animal skulls adorn the poles. Atop each is a ram's skull, and ribbons flutter from the horns. Difficult to tell, in the dark, but I'm certain the ribbons are all blue, red, or purple.

Garth halts. Fitzpatrick waits behind me.

"What now?" I ask.

Footfalls sound across the bridge, hollow and heavy, a man approaching. He stands taller than Garth, even ignoring his peculiar headdress, and by description I know what he is, though I've never seen anything like him with my own eyes.

Hide boots, deerskin leggings, leather tunic, bearskin mantle, a beaver-pelt headdress whose knotted-leather veil obscures the man's bearded face. Caribou antlers rise from his head. He carries a long spear, its point sufficient to skewer a horse.

A Horned Lord.

"Welcome to Threshold," he says, his tone soothing. "I admit it's not much to look at these days."

The baby quiets, burbles softly. I stroke the top of his head.

The Horned Lord asks, "What're you seeking?"

"The Queens."

"Why?"

"To join them."

"Why?"

"I heard of them in the east," I say. "I heard they're like no one else, like nothing the world has ever seen, that I might find safety here—"

He scoffs. "No such thing as *safety*. If that's what you're after, go somewhere else."

"Food, shelter, *some* security?" I caress the top of the baby's head. "Especially for this one, a chance to live."

With his left hand, the Horned Lord reaches for the baby's head. My first instinct is to pull away, but the Lord only caresses the little one's cheek.

The man's voice low but still gentle, as if he's speaking to the baby, he says, "Turn off your fucking headlamp."

I do. To my eyes, the darkness becomes nearly absolute. The Horned Lord leans close and his odor is herbal, medicinal, some blend of marshmallow root, mint, and pepper.

"Look at me," he says.

As I lift my chin, I guess his height near two meters. I wonder if he detects the tremble in my breath? The baby begins to cry, then quiets again, and the seconds grind on.

What does the Horned Lord see?

He chuckles. "To whom do you owe your allegiance?"

I could say *no one,* but I have a better lie. "Myself."

"What's your name?"

"Aur."

"What's your faith?" he asks me.

"I—I'm atheist."

True enough. Some call Mr. Avidità a God-King, but I never have, not as anything more than a metaphor—*Gods of the New Moons*—and metaphors aren't realities. Mr. Avidità was born, has lived, and is only as immortal as the technological singularity on which he surfs. There are no Gods.

Again, the chuckle. "All right, atheist, kneel."

"What?"

His voice becomes granite. "Kneel."

Though on my knees, I prepare to defend the infant. The Lord reaches into a pouch at his belt, digs his thumb into it, and in one smooth motion presses his thumb to my forehead.

The pain slams my eyes shut and empties my lungs. I grunt and double over, pressing my left hand to the earth, cradling the baby with my right, even in agony compelled to protect him. The flesh above the bridge of my nose burns and does *not* burn, the sensation like a cinder pressed to my skin.

No sizzling, though, no stink of ruined tissue.

Chemical maybe, something exciting the nerves, a drug.

I grit my teeth, the pain spreading across my skull. Endurable. Weakening until a migraine would be no worse. I allow myself a grunt, but I utter no words, no scream. The baby, perhaps sensing my pain, perhaps hating the way he's being held, perhaps wanting nothing more than a nap, shrieks.

"Tough motherfucker," says Fitzpatrick.

"Open your eyes," says the Horned Lord.

A chill of sweat spreads across my body. I straighten my back, fill my lungs, and the anger he reads on my face is real.

"What do you see, atheist?" He grins.

My focus remains on him. "An asshole."

He laughs.

At my periphery, Fitzpatrick and Garth glance at each other, then step back like they might from a wild bear—or an impending murder. The Horned Lord's rough laughter softens once more into a chuckle.

"All right, Aur," he says, "I have a camp, a fire, some *safety*. You and the child can stay there the night, rise in the morning, and be on your way to New Juneau."

Garth begins, "Hallowed, aren't you—"

The Horned Lord lifts his hand to silence the man. "Aur is our guest. As did the ancient Greeks, we should treat every strange *guest* as if he might be the Messenger of the Gods."

"Yes, Hallowed."

"In fact," the Lord says, "tomorrow I'll guide Aur to New Juneau myself."

X. SCIMITARS OF HEAVEN

Recollected
2116.6.24.14:05 GMT
2.3 AU from Sol
Inner Asteroid Belt
Africa IV

O N THE SECOND NIGHT in Africa IV, Mr. Avidità and I camped in a canvas tent, one like any tent of the nineteenth century. The evening had been so pleasant we'd rolled up the sides. In a radius around us, tiny drones maintained a perimeter, projecting high frequencies into the dark, too high for my ears but unpleasant for many animals.

Except the flies. The indefatigable flies.

Out in the darkness, Apollo and Ares stood guard.

"The flies," said Mr. Avidità, "part of an authentic experience."

I swatted them, waved at them, cursed at them. One committed suicide at the back of my throat.

"Be thankful," he said, "we've engineered the mosquitoes. Many birds and bats depend on the mozzies, but they're here in small numbers and seldom wander far from the river. No malaria, no dengue, no yellow fever. We get to sleep without nets."

"Thank you for bringing me," I said.

"You're welcome, Aur. For every creature here, we've got a thousand embryos on ice, but a biome is more than its DNA. The mammals and birds teach behaviors to their young, behaviors we'd lose if we iced the population. These animals," he said, "and the biomes in *all* the terraria—these are my Flapjacks."

I understood.

"How worried are you?" I asked. "About Nesteler?"

"Extremely."

A kilometer or two away, a lion roared. Somewhere a nightbird, whose species I did not know, called repeatedly.

"Are your defenses really in place?" I asked.

"No Rack can torture me," he said. "My Soul—at Liberty—

"Behind this mortal Bone

"There knits a bolder One—

"You cannot prick with saw—

"Nor pierce with Scimitar—"

"Emily Dickinson." I said.

He leaned back in his camp chair. "Each time *No Rack can torture me* comes to mind, I have to forgive her *pricking saw* and *piercing scimitar,* but her metaphors don't detract from her meaning. Dickinson was a stoic if there ever was one."

I scratched the back of my neck, shooing yet another fly. "Why Dickinson?"

"If I've directed the pieces upon the chessboard poorly, you and I will need what is *behind our mortal bone,* because we'll be dead within twenty-four hours."

I startled. "You're joking?" I said, instantly regretting those words.

Mr. Avidità seldom *joked* about anything.

He lit a small stove for water, then retrieved a satchel of tea and two cups. My namesake once wrote, *Concerning death, it is either a dispersion of atoms, a vanishing, an extinction, or a translation to another state.* Death made no difference to him.

"We're not *leaving?*" I asked.

Mr. Avidità's brows furrowed. "I'll need to respond to any battle in realtime, not delayed by light speed at a distance."

I wanted to yell, *What about me?!* But didn't dare.

"My scimitar will not *pierce,*" he said, "but I've poised it to swoop, to lop the heads from our enemies, to take them while they still imagine themselves the clever ones."

"What should I expect, Your Grace?"

"Nesteler's attack, like my defenses, will rely on AI, on heuristics and stochastics calculated in microseconds. Not much we can do while the AIs duke it out. Afterwards, though, if Nesteler's sent flesh-and-blood agents, we'll have to capture as many as we can—or kill them."

Insects sang or chanted rhythms, a wall of sound, and the lions roared for their territory. Mr. Avidità's water boiled, he steeped the tea, then handed me a cupful.

After sipping, I asked, "Your Grace, why *did* you bring me here?"

"I've gotten the sense you feel deeply for animals, Aur. Your sensitivity has always defined you, and I'm happy I didn't misread it. Would it upset you if this place, all the animals in it, were destroyed?"

My chest clenched. "Of course."

"Would it," he said, "if it disappeared, and you never got a chance to see it?"

I understood his point.

"We all die," he said, then he took a long draw of his tea, an excellent oolong. "Best to see the good stuff while you can."

Twenty hours later, I strapped myself back into the cockpit of the *Plato,* the trimaran still nestled in its docking bay. The centripetal force of Africa IV's rotation pressed me into my harness, without which I'd fly from my seat and smack into the windows. Mr. Avidità climbed into his seat, latched himself in, and rotated into viewing position.

A voice across the comm said, "This is *Alstad.*"

Mr. Avidità powered up the *Plato's* engines. "Go ahead, *Alstad.*"

"First hostiles crossing our Mesh in five, four, three, two—"

Across my field of vision, outside the *Plato's* diamondide ports, hundreds of faraway explosions flared into brilliant life, then winked back into darkness, some no brighter than the stars which provided their backdrop. This silent fireworks display carried on for seconds, at our flanks too, and from our position the explosions resembled mere firecrackers.

Each signified the destruction of a full-size attack drone, a striker, even a manned ship.

The comm crackled: "Electromagnetic jamming on both sides."

"Expected. Relay to my ansible if needed."

"Yes, sir."

An ansible? On the *Plato?*

Ansibles were rare devices, spooky chatterboxes at a distance. Ridiculously valuable.

The fireworks extravaganza continued.

"And we have a stray," said the *Alstad.*

A sliver of light arched toward the planetoid. Two or three hundred kilometers from Africa IV's surface, a nuclear warhead detonated, a spectacular blossom of pure photons. In reflex, I raised my arm to protect my eyes, but the *Plato's* AI reacted faster, darkening the viewports. A shockwave followed, translating into a low boom within the pressurized confines of our trimaran, a moment of rattle and shake.

"—number two—"

A similar close call, the comm reported, from the planetoid's other side. The Battle for Africa IV drew to a finish, the lights in the void growing infrequent.

"All incoming destroyed," came the report.

"*Alstad,*" said Mr. Avidità, "update your position."

Through the holovid the position appeared as pure data. "Moving in to sweep their approach."

"Happy hunting." Mr. Avidità smiled, let go a tense breath. "Do we have any incidental targets?"

"We have two."

"Two?" Mr. Avidità's smile faded. "Can you give me their trajectory?"

"Better, sir, we've cracked their stealth."

The *Plato* hummed to life and we detached from port. The cockpit's full holographic interface rendered and, though we still relied on the AIs, Mr. Avidità made manual adjustments, overrode safety constraints, armed weapons.

"Hang on, Aur, g-forces are going to get mean."

We peaked at *8.7,* the blood rushed from my head, and my vision narrowed. I managed, though, to remain conscious. The AIs calculated a multivariate intercept course to another ship, but at these speeds and in these conditions my all-too-human eye could spot nothing—

—then—

A tiny dot grew bigger, a larger vessel with more thrust but much more mass, some kind of troop or personnel carrier. Its thrusters over-burned as it dodged and wove, anticipating our targeting system.

"*Alstad,*" said Mr. Avidità, "think you can capture the other one? Take prisoners?"

The reply came, "Already on it."

My employer addressed his own ship's AIs: "Apollo, Ares, estimate our odds of commandeering the target vessel without casualty to me or to Aurelius."

The computers answered, "Eight-point-seven percent, plus or minus seven-point-two percent."

"Give me the odds of either of us dying if we engage to destroy."

"Five-point-two percent, plus or minus one-point-four percent."

He glanced at me. *"That* makes for a clear decision." To the AIs he said, "Bring us into engagement range."

The *Plato* accelerated at *4g,* gaining on our target. Firing controls rendered onto my holoscreen, above my lap, and the targeting system centered on the Nesteler transport.

"Take the shot," said Mr. Avidità. "Let's mark one up for the lions and elephants."

I'd never killed before, and for a first time that was a lot of killing. Yet much in the same way a short life mattered no less than a long one, killing many was no worse than killing one. My crèche brothers were earmarked as the executioners, as those who'd go for black-ops. Me, all I wanted was to get back to Flapjacks.

Though I didn't like it, I triggered the *Plato's* weapons.

XI. SOOTHSAYER

2131.4.10.5:44 PST
58°45'19.5"N 132°47'49.5"W
Alt 215m
British Columbia (Dissolved)
Stikine Region
111km to Destination

FOR MONTHS MY FIRST responsibilities have been to the baby, though nurses also attended his crèche, assisted by artificial intelligences. When you care for anything, day after day, the caring changes you, tunes your deepest fibers to a more orderly Brownian frequency. When he's hungry, I feed him; when uncomfortable, I accommodate him; when thirsty, I give him water. When he cries, I comfort him. When the baby wakes, I awaken too, even when I'm exhausted.

This frosty predawn is no different. I change him—inside the tent, twice as unpleasant, but I want him warm as possible. After he's wiped, I swaddle him, then climb outside to deposit the old diaper.

Beside the embers of last night's fire, the Horned Lord sits. He watches the purplish eastern sky, the fading stars, the shine of Venus and Jupiter above the treetops.

After returning to the tent I set the stove, under the rainfly's awning, for both tea and formula. Somewhere out of sight, either Garth or Fitzpatrick snores. I manage to enjoy my tea while feeding the baby and, blessedly, he slumbers. My view frames the Lord where he remains by the fire pit. In the growing light, his clothing's blue and vermillion stains grow vibrant. At first I think to watch the sunrise with him, but before long my eyelids droop.

I set aside the teacup and close up the tent.

I WAKE BECAUSE I'M hot, Sol blazing and high through the tent's carbon-nylon fabric. Almost ten o'clock. With a start I sit, terrified the baby might be gone, that he might be dead. Yet he sleeps beside me, peaceful, his limbs splayed with his tiny hands by his head, his face turned, his slender lips puckered.

I climb from the tent, run my hands through my hair, and rub the sleep from my eyes. Garth's and Fitzpatrick's tents stand a dozen meters apart from mine. I don't know which is which, or which contains the pack now holding my gun and ammunition. The Horned Lord's oiled-leather tent displays decorations and iconographies I don't understand. A pole rises beside it, ringed by bird feathers and rodent skulls. At its top, a human jawbone resembles a prong, affixed with dried tendon. The fire crackles low. On a stone beside it rests a tall pot, which Garth tends.

"That can't be coffee," I say, "can it?" We have coffee on Station, but reports suggested its presence here would be unlikely.

"Roots and herbs," says Garth, eyeing me. "Pretty good, but I *do* miss coffee."

Across the camp, nearer the river, Fitzpatrick pees on a wild rosebush. The Horned Lord appears nowhere.

"I didn't mean to sleep so long," I say.

"You needed it," says Garth.

"I guess so."

"Fitz and me, we haven't minded a slow morning either."

"What happened last night?" I point to my forehead. "What the fuck was that?"

Garth drops his head, won't quite meet my eye. He pours some of the hot liquid into a steel cup, then hands it to me. Its bitterness hits the back of my tongue, followed by a spiciness, analogous to cinnamon.

"What happened," he says, almost whispering, "is you should be dead."

"Why?"

He shakes his head. "What you felt there, last night, that was a Questioning."

"A Questioning?"

"That pain is what happens when someone *lies* to a Horned Lord."

"Lies?"

"Something about what you told him wasn't true, and the Horned Lords, they *hate* it when people lie to them."

"Most people do."

Garth says, "When someone lies to a Horned Lord," then he draws his thumb across his throat.

"I see."

But I *don't* see, don't understand how a chemically induced headache could correspond with my mistruths, have never heard of any polygraph like it. Fitzpatrick returns to the fire. In the daylight he reminds me of a fuzzy river otter, his body and neck too long for his arms and legs. His prominent Adam's apple bobs when he swallows, and he waves me toward him.

As I sit with him, he unpacks a bundled cloth, wrapped around knobby contents which rattle when he shakes them. He unties the bundle, lays down the cord, then flattens the cloth, a square bigger than a bandana, brocade with silver fabric. The cloth spills its contents—ten bones, the size of chicken femurs.

Not chicken femurs. Human phalanges or metacarpus bones.

The brocade marks out a five-by-five grid, and Fitzpatrick scatters the bones over it. They tumble, laying against each other, and he reads their pattern like an engineer might interpret an electrical diagram. To find so much superstition amongst these survivors of the Pacific Northwest is no surprise, not given what I have read, and I indulge it.

"What do they say?" I ask.

"That I'm sharing the campfire with a zombie." He giggles.

"Zombie?"

"Isn't that what they call the living dead?"

"I feel quite alive today."

Still no sign of the Horned Lord. Garth sets out a blanket, begins to disassemble his rifle, organizes a cleaning kit. The sun feels grand, though western clouds are already rolling inland.

"All the undead," says Fitzpatrick, "at first they're confused."

"What do you mean?"

"Till someone proves to them they're dead, they insist they're alive. The mind, you see, it can't handle the idea of death."

I keep his logical inconsistencies to myself. "What else do your bones say?"

"This pattern is *the bridge.*" He points to a configuration where three bones touch one another. Two rest wholly inside their squares, while the third intersects a silvered line. "You bring worlds together, baby-zombie-man."

"Explain."

He draws his finger over the configuration. "This here means *the heavens,* and this means *the earth.* I don't know, maybe you're grounded but also visionary? Or unrealistic? Or fanciful?"

"I don't think of myself as any of those things."

His giggle peters out. "Well, it ain't a science."

He's got that right.

His Adam's apple wobbles. "When your death comes," he says, "it'll be horrible. But it'll be worth it."

The breeze shifts and campfire smoke rolls past us. The baby's voice demands my attention.

"I'll keep that in mind," I say.

"Keep it in mind or not," he says, gathering his bones, retying the cloth, "won't make no difference."

I shift my weight, ready to stand, but Fitzpatrick grabs my arm. His whisper is serious, sharp: "Next time a Horned Lord asks you what you see, try to say something better than *an asshole.*"

"I'll keep that in mind too."

From the north the Horned Lord reenters camp, using his long spear as a walking stick. He marches to the fire and tosses a human hand into it. Fitzpatrick scrambles back, his attention locked on the appendage, and I too retreat. Garth looks up from his rifle maintenance.

"You two," says the Lord to the men, "pack up and head back out. The Queens have ordered the border closed. For now the Faen is shut."

Neither man asks about the hand. They hurry to obey, all other thoughts abandoned. The baby's cry rises.

"Care for your little ward," the Horned Lord says to me. "When you're ready, we'll be on our way."

XII. SURVEILLANCE
[OR, INTELLIGENCE, PART I]

Recollected
2130.9.19.12:41 GMT
Alt 40.2E6m
High Earth Orbit
EIK-Cel Station

I STOOD WITH MR. Avidità on an observation platform. Our orbit brought us over Earth's western hemisphere, a day-lit North America facing us, framed in my view by meters-tall windows of layered diamondide. My employer wore a tailored suit of spun silk, his tie patterned in yellows and blues reminiscent of fallen Sweden, and his cufflinks bore the likeness of Queen Christina.

"The region around New Juneau, Alaska," he said. "Look. You don't need a telescope, needn't bother with the satellites."

A mottled, diseased patchwork of browns, yellows, and greens, the Americas reminded me of old, discolored photographs, not of geography but of twentieth-century cancer victims in the hours before their deaths. I studied the Alaskan coastline, the way I might study a puzzle or an illusion. My intake of breath was audible, unintentional.

"You see it?" he asked.

Faint, indistinct, but now I detect what the AIs must have identified a year ago or more. In a sweeping arc, reaching inland, the *color*—

"Green," I said, "and—"

"You *see* it?"

"A shade of violet."

"Spectrography caught it first," he said, "but now it's distinct enough for the naked eye. We expect, after another decade, it'll be obvious to anyone with functional pupils, and it keeps growing."

"What is it?"

"No fucking idea."

"Your Grace?"

"No fucking idea. Biotech? Nanotech? Both? Something we don't understand yet. We've collected plants, soil, birds, small mammals, pollen."

"No conclusion?"

"Not one promising goddamned hypotheses. Just—"

"What, sir?"

He shares anecdotal reports about the Horned Lords, tales of the superstitious north, accounts out of Prince George. He tells me of two women who lived awhile in San Francisco, of their strange condition, and of their violent departure.

"You say their trackers never switched off?" I asked.

"They haven't moved either."

"Where are they?"

"Wrangell Island."

"The trackers have been there the *whole* time?"

He nodded. "My guess? Bettina and Cailín removed them soon after arriving in the Panhandle, but they've preserved them."

"Why?"

"To taunt me?" he said, thinking on it. "Or tempt me."

"What did their tissue samples tell us?"

"Remarkable resiliency, resistance to cancer, immunity to most bacteria, robust telomeres. Damndest thing I've ever seen. But no identifiable pathogen, nothing which should've been communicable. It was as if Bettina Ukweli's cells had been engineered in the best lab money can buy. Nesteler's labs. UPRC's labs. But hell no, she was born in goddamn Winnipeg to an ordinary family, unusual for its genetic diversity, but solidly working class. No more *designed* than a common titmouse."

"Unusual for its genetic diversity?"

"Her maternal grandmother was Kenyan. Maternal great grandfather, Chinese. Her paternal grandfather immigrated from Pakistan in twenty forty-three, then married her paternal grandmother, who was Quebecois and as caucasian as they come." He chuckled. "Young Bettina was a poster child for multiracial harmony. 'Kumbaya'. 'We Are the World'. Et cetera."

"What about the unidentifiable pathogen, Your Grace? It *shouldn't have been* communicable, you said, but it was."

"Most definitely." Again he nodded. "Sexually transmitted."

"Bettina and Cailín both carried it?"

"Near as we could tell, Cailín gave it to Bettina, but it spread no further, not in San Francisco."

"It bothers you to see puzzles unsolved."

"We need to know what's happening in the Pacific Northwest, why the hell our satellites aren't registering everything they should, why our field drones don't come back."

That surprises me. "We have no drone observations of New Juneau?"

"Few, and none of Wrangell."

"What about our spies?"

"I've learned not to send anyone with high technology. All the transmitters, imbedded sensors, or sensory augmentation don't help. Our spies go in but—" His words trailed off.

"We've lost them all?"

"All but one."

"He have *any* insights?"

"She did. Three main points. First, the Queens' rule inside their growing circle appears absolute. Second, superstition and religious zealotry define the society they're building."

"What kind of superstition?"

"They worship a God named *Nodens.*"

"The Celtic deity?"

"Who they call the Horned Lord." Mr. Avidità shrugged. "Our agent has spoken of uncivilized rites, hedonism, human sacrifice—"

"Terrible."

"Her last insight, though, was the most interesting."

"What was it?"

"The Queens have a soft spot. They forbid the harming of children, and they adopt every young orphan who comes to them."

Forbid the harming? I couldn't help but compare such an idea to my own experiences.

"Every bit of intelligence we have on Bettina Ukweli and Cailín Byrne," he said, "read it."

"Yes, Your Grace."

"I have a mission for you, one that could decide the future of System."

For a moment I couldn't breathe. "I'm your man."

"Good. It'll take us several months to prepare."

"In the meantime I'll study everything I can, whatever you see fit. Perhaps I could begin by interviewing our surviving spy?"

Mr. Avidità faced me. The Earthshine lit his profile.

"You're welcome to," he said. "Her name is Cassandra Watson, if you want to look her up, but I'm afraid she won't do you much good."

"Why not?"

"Because these days she mostly gibbers and drools. Despite our best efforts at treating her, you see, she's completely lost her mind."

XIII. THE HUNGRY

2131.4.11.19:10 PST
58°43'16.5"N 133°25'05.6"W
Alt 5m
British Columbia (Dissolved)
Stikine Region
79km to Destination

THOUGH MORE SLOWLY, THE Horned Lord walks as many hours as I would, and by yesterday evening we'd covered twenty-seven klicks. A wide, well-maintained path eases our way and, whenever we cross marshland, pylon-constructed boardwalks accommodate us. In most of a second day we've pushed another thirty-two klicks, passing the confluence of the Inklin River and the Taku, a bigger drainage which rolls to the Tulsequah Inlet and New Juneau.

The baby hates this and the poor little guy's nearing his limit. Yet infants survived the Stone Age, the neolithic, and early history, and they're tougher than many believe. He shrieks for the better part of two hours, and I find myself worrying the Horned Lord's patience will break, that to silence the baby he'll attempt something horrific.

Yet he says, "Children *are* a gift." Not a hint of cliché, irony, or unconsidered habit.

Evening approaches and, to the west, Sol has disappeared behind the Boundary Peaks. Nearer the coast, they grow taller, young mountains prone to earthquakes. Even in this warming world, snow covers their crowns, the remnants of glaciers. The air, hot throughout the afternoon, once more grows cold.

Ahead, stretched across the entire valley, appears some kind of wall. In the half-light, its dull gray almost escapes my attention, but from kilometers away I can tell it's *big*, at least a dozen meters high.

"What's that?" I ask.

"The Bonlin," replies the Horned Lord.

As we near it, I've the impression of a masonry structure, stones stacked in endless numbers. Dark spots mottle the masonry's gray but, as we approach closer still, that illusion falls away. I stop.

"Jesus fucking Christ."

With a howl of laughter, the Horned Lord says, "I thought you said you were an atheist."

"I am."

The Bonlin spans the width of the valley, crossing the river in an impressive arc, supported on pylons. A single gatehouse allows the road to pass. The gates stand open and, above them, men guard the wall. Constructed of concrete, stone, razor wire, and human bones, I can only imagine the Bonlin exists foremost to terrify.

It is, more than a defensive barrier, a monument to death.

Row after countless row of skulls stare east, across the valley, the most macabre of construction materials cemented into a gargantuan barrier. The skulls sit upon femurs, tibias, fibulas, ribs, pelvises, spines, ulnas, radiuses, and humeri. Like the catacombs of Paris, vomited into the Yukon landscape.

"How many *are* there?" I ask.

"Bones?"

"Skulls."

"In *this* wall?" The Lord grunts. "Tens of thousands."

"There's more than one wall?"

"Several, on key routes."

"So goddamned many," I say.

"How many unburied dead on Earth?" he asks. "Billions?"

"Yes."

"This," he says, sweeping his arm to indicate the Bonlin. "This is *nothing.*"

Without word we cross the gates, and the guards watch us go by. Among them stand Horned Lords in their red and blue leathers, with their wild beards, wearing their distinguishing antlers. Once we reach the other side, the gates close, and in half an hour we round another bend in the river. Passing behind a ridge, I lose sight of the Bonlin.

I am now inside the realm of the Queens—the Faen—and I wonder if I'll ever again leave it.

In a dry meadow beside the Taku, the Lord and I stop for the night. While I tend the baby, the Horned Lord builds a fire in an old pit. Soon it blazes, casting an inviting light into the chilly evening. To the south, owls hoot to one another. The clouds thicken and the golden sunsets, bright stars, and scintillating Milky Way will make no appearance tonight. The Moon, waxing gibbous, provides a silvery backdrop, a bright southerly smear. I bundle the baby to me, sit nearer the fire, and prepare my own food.

The Horned Lord unwraps several lengths of dried meat and, as he chews, he stares at me across the flames. "You frightened?"

"Should I be?" I ask.

He shrugs. "You crossed Canada?"

"A good portion of it."

"Coming from?"

"Up from Minnesota." My lies are practiced and five layers deep. They drop easily from me, though I remember Fitzpatrick's warnings. This time, though, no headaches strike me down. "There was a community there—"

"Trying to rebuild."

"Yeah."

With his teeth he tears another mouthful of jerky, speaks while he eats. "Idiots."

"You don't think people should try rebuilding? Make a go of it?"

"Anyone still outside the Faen should avail themselves of one of the many firearms still available on Earth, chamber a single cartridge, and put a bullet through their own heads."

My revulsion is a sham, but I play it out. "There're so few of us left. If we could stop the violence, work together—"

"Barely *any* humans left! You're right about that, man-who-can't-possibly-be-from-Minnesota."

"I was born in Colorado."

"Explains your boring accent." Another bite, he grinds it between his molars. "But not your stupidity."

I shovel several mouthfuls of reconstituted beef and potatoes into my belly.

"Humans are all but gone," he says, snapping his fingers. "In a blink, ten billion to a pittance. But you know what's happening while the bones of those billions are bleaching out? Climate change marches on. Methane's seeping from Siberia, Greenland, and the Pacific. Unchecked, it will rise for ten thousand more years. The oceans will overheat apace, and the skies will get wetter, water vapor trapping more heat. Acidification will continue, adding to the feedback loop. Around the world, nuclear reactors are melting down, unattended as they are. Wildfires rage on. Whoever's left can 'stop the violence' and 'work together,' but Earth is poisoned. In a few thousand years, the destruction will make the Great Dying of the Permian look, well, like a mild culling. *Unchecked,* if Earth doesn't end up looking like Venus, at the least it's back to single-celled organisms. Might be a few hundred millions years before anything new develops a *backbone.*"

I sit back, swallow hard. The man before me resembles an ancient witch doctor, his beard grizzled, the bizarre purple stains at his lips hinting at something prehuman. Yet he speaks clearly, eloquently, assuredly.

"Whose hand was that?" I ask. "The one you threw into the fire?"

"A thief's, a man I'd been hunting awhile."

"What did he steal?"

"Food."

"Seems reasonable. A lot of starving down here this last decade."

He eyes me at *down here,* and I regret the choice in words. I keep eating, letting it slide, knowing they're words an Earthling might still have chosen.

The Horned Lord tears another length of jerky, grinds it between his molars. "First lesson—you've entered the Faen, and here no one steals food. You need food, you ask, and we figure out how to feed you. You steal food, there're penalties to pay. You *run,* the penalties are worse."

My MRE includes a chocolate brownie. I unwrap it, bite off the corner. "What about those poor evangelical assholes you skewered at the head of the Inklin Valley?"

"False prophecy," he said, "is a worse crime than thievery. There are only two High Priestesses here, only one priesthood. No others."

"And only one God?" The brownie isn't bad, the flavor of chocolate lingering. I shove the last of it into my mouth.

"No, atheist, there're *many* Gods, and Nodens resides between us and them. The Gods are all around us. Don't you feel them? Can't you see their signs?"

"I've never believed in fairytales."

He *tsks*. "You're stubborn, atheist."

"I admit, you're not what I expected of a Horned Lord."

After rewrapping the remainder of his jerky and putting it away, he gazes at me, resting his forearms on his knees. "What had you expected?"

"Lawless, thoughtless, uneducated, unpredictable heathens. You're a superstitious lot, but you're not wild animals."

He grunts, tilts his head. "You're not all wrong."

"No?"

"Heathen. That I'll own up to."

I throw the MRE box into the fire. Cardboard and plastic hiss and ignite.

"But you're *very* wrong on one account," says the Horned Lord.

"Oh?"

"We're *all* wild animals here," he says, "even you."

THE BABY GRANTED ME another full night's rest, but we're up at dawn and, after a feeding and change, we're on the move. As the sun rises we reach a parting in the road, and the end of the Taku, its mouth sixty-six meters higher than a hundred years ago. The river rolls slowly and broadly—almost a kilometer between its banks—but there's no silty delta, the river trapped between steep mountainsides in either direction, and it empties into a brackish inlet whose rocky banks mark the high tides.

Tulsequah.

From this nexus it's still impossible to spot the Admiralty and Angoon Islands, but they stand in the same salty waters no more than a hundred kilometers southwest. Beyond them are the Chicagof Islands, the Baranof Islands, then the Pacific. There're more tree-blanketed islands along this coast than before the Pulses which drowned the world, after the melting of Greenland and Antarctica, and updated surveys of these islands do not exist.

Two centuries ago, glaciers dominated these basins, but nowadays the ice accumulates and thaws seasonally. A thousand meters up, the mountaintops remain white with this last winter's snow. Where the river spills into the salt water, a series of docks look no more than a few years old. No boats at them, though, so I'm unsurprised when the Horned Lord follows the road away from the water, forking from the valley onto a forested mountainside. As we climb, the air freezes and I cradle the baby to my chest.

In our ascent we rest only once. Adjacent to the road, ravens flutter in the pines. There're ravens in the Avidità Terraria, but these Faen birds grow *much* larger than any I've ever seen. One stretches its wings, big as an eagle.

The Horned Lord caws at them, seems to converse with them, then we move on.

Six hundred meters up, the road levels and follows the mountains' contours. The slopes to our left drop steeply into the inlet. Twice more we pause, long enough to tend the baby, but we're making excellent time.

The scent of campfire smoke tickles my nose.

Around a bend appears a makeshift camp of seventeen adults, most no more than twenty years old, twelve men and five women. They carry rifles, handguns, and various blades. When they spot the Horned Lord, their conversations quiet.

The eldest among them addresses the Horned Lord: "Hallowed."

"A Reckoning," replies the Lord.

Dropping to their knees, these people bow. The fire crackles. At the edge of the camp, two donkeys graze on fresh spring grasses. In the distance, following us, the ravens continue their chatter.

"What're you doing?" the Horned Lord asks.

The eldest answers. "We've been hunting, Hallowed."

"Looks like a sad, shitty hunt."

No carcasses, no racks of meat, none smoking over the fires. A sullenness hangs over the group, their eyes a bit too sunken, their shoulders too low. Frustrated.

"Where does the land lead you?" the Lord asks them.

"We try to read the signs," says the eldest, "but it's hard."

"Nodens *guides* us. He doesn't shovel the food into our mouths—" The Lord points at the baby strapped to my chest. "—doesn't wipe our asses for us either. Listen to the land, the breath of Nodens as it swims over the earth, the movements of every living thing."

"Yes, Hallowed."

"The deer and elk have moved east, children, and you'll not find many this side of the Taku. Cross the river where you can, head southeast, and *hear* Nodens's breath."

"Yes, Hallowed."

"Come back to New Juneau with meat enough to feed twice your number for a fortnight."

"Yes, Hallowed."

"If you come back empty-handed," says the Horned Lord, "I'll butcher one of you myself, roast you to perfection, and feed you to anyone hungry enough to keep you down."

The hunting party answers, "Yes, Hallowed."

"Now, everyone, gather round."

All seventeen encircle him. I remain on the road, taking a moment to unstrap the baby, cradle him, and let him suckle on my finger.

"Hold up your hands," says the Lord to the hunters, and he demonstrates with his own hands as if to scoop water.

He unslings his heavy leather pack and draws from it a parcel of salted meat. He distributes large pieces, laying the morsels in every outstretched palm. As I watch him the hairs along my nape stand on end, my breath catches, and I absorb the details.

I cannot be seeing what I'm seeing.

The parcel is fat, the strips thick, maybe three kilos' worth of food. But enough to feed seventeen? No, in no way.

Strip after strip he lays on their palms until he fills every hand. Half a kilo each? A kilo? *More food than he can possibly have.* It's legerdemain, a common illusionist's trick, the same as pulling a rabbit from a hat.

Isn't it?

Designed to impress the superstitious.

At last he tells them, "That's all I have." He shows them his empty hands, as a party clown might reveal his spread fingers to a roomful of children.

The Horned Lord continues down the road, and he waves for me to follow. As I pass the hunters, they stare at me, their expressions weighted with envy, mistrust, and fear.

The Lord hastens, and we leave the hungry behind.

XIV. INFANT

Recollected
2131.1.3.11:17 GMT
Alt 40.1E6m
High Earth Orbit
EIK-Cel Station

"H E'S BEAUTIFUL," I SAID to Mr. Avidità, cradling the newborn in my arms, uncertain how to hold him, afraid I might break him.

Mr. Avidità and I sat in comfortable couches beside the Station Sector's nursery. Beyond its glass wall, nurses and robots alike looked after the well-being of a dozen infants, all identical ages, having slid from their artificial wombs within minutes of one another. Crèche mates, as I and my "brothers" had been.

"This child is different from the others," said Mr. Avidità.

As engineered individuals, crèche-born are both *more* alike and *less* alike than standard humans are from one another. Much of our DNA follows identical pattens, tried-and-true qualities worth repeating, but in other ways we exist for customization.

My employer continued, "For the next eleven weeks, you'll be with the baby every day, six hours a day. Six days per week, I want you training—long-distance running, endurance, combat, survival, infiltration. Skills you already have, but we need you at peak performance."

"Understood."

"This is the most important task I've ever asked of you, Aur."

"Thank you, Your Grace."

I caressed the infant's cheek. So tiny, only 3.1 kilos, half the weight he'd be by the time I found myself crossing into Alaska with a Horned Lord of the Faen.

"Mr. Avidità, what is it that makes *this* child so special? What is it you've created?"

"If you're captured, Aur, if you're tortured—"

"I understand, sir."

"I *will* suggest this to you—look into the baby's eyes."

A particular gray-green hue, clear and bright as the eyes of children tend to be. I studied them.

"Do you see it?" asked Mr. Avidità.

"They're *your* eyes, Your Grace, almost." His were darker, a deeper tint, as adults' often are. "The hue is identical."

"You've always been quick, always observant, always a caretaker."

"I try."

The baby's scent reminded me of Flapjacks.

"You are," said Mr. Avidità, "perfect for this mission."

I rocked the baby, more comfortable with him by the minute, with the feel of him next to me. "Thank you, Your Grace. I won't disappoint you."

Mr. Avidità clasped his hand against my shoulder, so paternal. "How could you ever disappoint me, Aur? I'm sure you never will."

AFTER MY FIRST TIME with the baby, I wandered the discuses and a couple of the more crowded parts of Station, amongst all the humans who'd once been Earthlings but who now lived in orbit, these people trying to rearrange their existences, to untether themselves from the grounds upon which they'd once survived. Most on EIK-Cel were North American, but of course North America had already been a hodgepodge of different peoples who sometimes got along and who sometimes didn't.

On Station, mostly, they got along. I operated on the theory that EIK-Cel's residents understood King Avidità's power, knew they lived in *his* house at *his* pleasure.

What a remarkable thing it was that Mr. Avidità had brought together so many traumatized people and that, so far, he had made it work. But on that day, the cosmopolitan peace was not what I most noticed.

Ever come to appreciate something for the first time, then you encounter it *everywhere?* A popular song, a famous painting, a bit of pop culture—something which was always there, but you'd never paid attention before. Now, once you notice it, you can't *not* notice it.

After holding the baby, I saw babies everywhere. I saw pregnant women *all over the place.*

Before Blight, before the Pulses, what percentage of North American women were pregnant at any given time? I'd never seen the statistics, didn't bother looking them up after that day, but it can't have been as many as were pregnant on Station. A fifth of women in their child-bearing years? A quarter?

An *insane* number of women.

I wondered why.

Was the answer anthropological? Something to do with having survived the traumas of the last few years and now finding themselves in relative safety?

Was the answer evolutionary? Something engrained in humans which, after a catastrophic collapse of population, raises fertility rates?

I never answered the question. In the months preceding my mission, I'd simply been too busy to follow my curiosity.

XV. VISIONS, PART V

T HE RAIN SLAPS MY face, seeping heat from my breath, my throat, my chest, leaving me trembling. I work the ship's rudder, steering into the wind, forcing us perpendicular to the relentless, titanic waves. Their foam-flecked black waters arch like beasts, hateful dragons, and each time our ship's prow climbs vertical, the angry clouds confront me. Lightning knifes them, leaving impossible afterimages—elephantine rams whose gigantic horns spiral through the mists, rams yoked to a war chariot, rams driven by a God whose hammer sparks fire.

The wave drops and our clinker vessel slams down with it, traversing the waterscape, the living mountains of brine and slithering valleys of foam. By each gunwale, a dozen men row, two to an oar, a dozen oars beating the surface again, again, again. These men, bred for the waves, their muscles sculpted for this work, they shake off the storm, their only purpose to carry us through it.

Some wear the antlers of the Horned Lords.

Husbands to the Queens.

At the prow stands a boy, ten or eleven years old, fair-haired and steady. The rain lashes him but does not bend him. Once more, lightning thrashes the sky, the ship cresting a wave only to rush downward again.

The boy looks over his shoulder at me, at the men. "Forward!" he screams, his voice carrying over the thunder.

Another swell, and for a heartbeat we hang weightless, risk capsizing. The ship groans, its rivets sing, and the men grunt with every pull. We mount the wave and tilt forward, gazing into an inky maelstrom.

"Ph'nglui mglw'nafh," the boy cries out, a thunder crash muffling his words, "wgah'nagl fhtagn!"

His peculiar gray-green eyes reflect the lightning.

From the maelstrom emerges a grotesquerie carved from nightmares and wrongnesses, a waxy and leathery expansiveness of blubbery masses, of pseudopods, of innumerable eyes. Its jet flesh glistens and, in the wet reflection of thunderbolts, it uncoils from the abyss and transfixes us in its multitudinous gaze. Its chest-shaking shriek deafens me to the cascading thunder.

Its writhing bulk lifts from the water, dwarfing our ship, the waves, the maelstrom, until the lightning-thorned clouds become its crown. Its stink pollutes the winds but, more profound, its otherworldliness rolls stingingly across our vessel.

Toxic to life.

Offensive to our senses.

Poisonous to our thoughts.

It is a *mind,* and its mind crushes ours.

Its eyes penetrate me, probe me, scour me inside-out. Is that me screaming? Is the warmth between my legs my urine? I release the rudder and our ship flounders.

The grotesquerie lifts us into the sky. One man leaps overboard, vanishes. Others cry or cower. The Horned Lords lift their spears and attempt some formation.

"Cthulhu nei fhtagn!" shouts the boy.

This Great Old One splinters the ship and I am—

　　—falling—

　　　　—forever.

§

2131.4.12.5:12 PST
58°16'06.8"N 134°10'11.6"W
Alt 376m
Southeast Alaska (Dissolved)
Tongass
18km to Destination

WITH A GASPING BREATH I wake.

The baby still sleeps.

A sense of drowning passes from me, a fading and fevered dream. A Harque seldom forgets, but this dream slides from me, fish-slippery, desperate to wriggle from my brain and return to the currents of my subconsciousness.

Hot sweat coats me and I unzip my sleeping bag, craving cooler air. Sol remains below the horizon, but the sky has lightened to a ubiquitous gray.

Rain pelts the tent. For more than twenty-four hours, rainstorms have doused the mountains and forests, the drainages rush with water, and the skies roil with shades of slate and charcoal. The deluge sharpens the scents of pine and fern, and the entire land *smells* alive.

While still sheltered, I tend the baby, set the dirty diaper outside, and manage a feeding. The supply of formula is dwindling but still ample. At least my backpack is getting lighter. Lotion, talc, and medicines are in good order. The poor little guy's thighs are red, and today I'll try carrying him differently.

In the rain there's no clean way to pack. The best I can do is attempt to keep mud from the tent's interior. By the time I've bundled everything, the day has brightened as much as it's likely to, and the Horned Lord awaits, his gear on his back. He leans on his long spear while rain pours through his hair, beads across his face, and soaks his beard.

"Ready?" he asks.

I nod.

To the southeast, hundreds of meters down, the Taku Inlet peeks through a fog. *Taku,* named by the Tlingit tribe who once lived here, before the Americans, before the Russians. I don't know if there are any Tlingit left alive. I hope there are.

Today, the Horned Lord and I will round a promontory at the southwest foot of Mt. Roberts. The going will be slow but, by nightfall, we'll have dropped nearer the Gastineau Channel and, with any luck, we'll cross by ferry to Douglas Island.

To New Juneau.

Before we rejoin the road, I adjust my pack and cradle the baby's side against my chest. He's suckling a pacifier, and I keep him close, sharing my warmth. Louder than the rain, the cawing of ravens echoes through the forest, and twice more I spot that eagle-sized specimen.

The Horned Lord says, "That's Nevermore." He laughs. "You're blessed, atheist, that he should show *any* interest in you."

The bird takes wing, joins his kin, and disappears into the fog.

"Why?" I ask.

"Because Nevermore is the Queens' familiar."

"Like a witch's pet?"

He grunts, though whether deriding me or agreeing, I can't tell.

"If they didn't already know you're here, atheist, they do now."

Then I notice, obvious as it is, for the first time—the darkened, saturated, rain-soaked green of the forest overlies an even darker color.

Violet.

Everywhere, so subtle but ubiquitous as to have been rendered transparent, perhaps invisible in the dry conditions of the last few days. The rains reveal it.

It shimmers through the forest's dappled emeralds and browns. I've never experienced this color before, not in any digital imagery, not in the natural spectra of any biome in any terraria managed by the Avidità Corporation. I crouch by the roadside and run my fingertips across a growth of fireweed, let two leaves rest against my pale fingertips.

Over several minutes, the leaves grow visibly, by millimeters.

"This isn't possible," I say.

In this downpour the woodland stretches and reaches, whispering as it does, creeping more like a slow animal than any vegetation. How does this biome process carbon so rapidly? Where does the nitrogen come from? Neither the laws of thermodynamics nor any biological theory accounts for *this much* growth so quickly.

The Horned Lord moseys down the road. "Keep telling yourself that, atheist. Come on. This day will be over before you know it."

XVI. IT'S ALL WARS

Recollected
2131.2.14.4:22 GMT
Alt 40.0E6m
High Earth Orbit
EIK-Cel Station

B RINGING ROSES IN A glass vase, that seemed a kind gesture to me. Despite their fleeting existence, there's a lasting poetry in roses:

The soft beauty of their petals. A soothing pink, in this case.

The hard sharpness of their thorns.

The pleasure of their scent.

It'd been years since I'd reason to be at Station's medical discus. In my youth it was my own broken bones and lacerations which necessitated such visits, often after tussles with my crèche brothers.

The discus's lower levels housed offices for routine visits, wellness exams, and urgent care. With few exceptions, AIs administered residents' diagnostics, traced epidemiological trends, and managed scheduling, but the need for interpersonal connection remained, and doctors provided a valuable check-sum to the AIs' overall system.

I bypassed these levels, glancing at everyday people as they waited for their appointments. In Station's controlled environs, few injuries required long-term attention but prevention mattered more than ever. Everyone saw their doctor at least twice per year.

Communicable diseases posed the greatest risks.

A lift brought me to the higher levels, where I walked by facilities which grew organs for transplants, which housed vacuum-sterile surgical theaters, which directed some of Avidità Corporation's medical experiments. On these levels, too, a handful of mental-healthcare facilities housed patients whose conditions puzzled the most advanced twenty-second-century technologies.

The facility's chief medical officer, Dr. Tulaja Chowdhury, met me. From her file I knew her to be sixty-eight years old, though she passed for early thirties. She shook my hand, her demeanor affable, welcoming, and professional. Her offices were clean, inviting, and tastefully designed, with touches of Hindu decor—a sculpture of the Goddess Parvati, a procession of Asian elephants carved from sisso wood, a tapestry depicting the epics of Ganesh.

"Mr. Aurelius, it's a pleasure to receive you."

I smiled but shook my head. "Aurelius will do, no *mister* necessary. Thank you. I realize my request is unusual."

"Not at all. *Any* requests from Mr. Avidità's representatives are our duty. We're here because of him."

"Thank you."

"Ms. Watson is particularly lucid today. You're in luck." Dr. Chowdhury's attention shifted to the bouquet, whose vase I tucked against my left side. "What are those?"

"Roses."

"I know what they are, Aurelius, but what do you *intend* to do with them?"

"Ms. Watson's file indicated she likes roses. I thought they might make a friendly gesture."

"You cannot take the glass in with you."

"All right."

"I'm afraid I can't let you give her the stems either."

Dr. Chowdhury stepped back from me, studying me like a fashion designer might study a runway model. "None of your clothes are appropriate. Your belt, your shoes, the heavy fabric of your pants."

"Why?"

"For example, your belt—woven fiber, isn't it?"

"Hydroponic cotton," I said, proud because it'd come from a facility which I helped manage. "Grown in narrow-spectrum darkrooms, not a gram of water or nitrogen lost in the system."

"Good for you," said the doctor. "If Cassandra gets hold of it, there's a chance she'll strangle you with it. Or me. Or she'll hang herself."

"You're kidding?"

"I'm not," she said. "We've got to get you out of your clothes."

Cassandra Watson's living space fit inside a volume seven meters square by 2.5 meters tall. Along one wall, tucked into a raised space, was her bed. Beside it the bathroom had no door and no privacy. One entire wall, being clear diamondide, looked into an alluringly tended garden to which Ms. Watson had no physical access.

I entered wearing what amounted to gossamer underwear and a T-shirt, printed from fabric which anyone could shred. Dr. Chowdhury had reduced the bouquet of roses to their pink petals, which I carried in a water-soluble plastic bowl.

As I stepped through the security lock into Ms. Watson's domicile, she stood from the floor. She'd been sitting on a cushion, facing her garden. Holograms of her had depicted a thin, birdlike woman with dark eyes and long, sable hair. In person, her hair was shorn within a centimeter of her scalp.

"I appreciate your kind gesture," she said.

I held out the petals for her. She took the bowl, then in handfuls scattered the contents around her apartment. The petals starkly contrasted the pale carpet, which resembled tatami, though the material was a woven carbon which would be almost impossible to rip from the floor, to unwind, or to burn. Every item in this space, I realized, was either so tough as to be immovable or so frail as to be harmless.

After she'd stippled the floor in petals, Ms. Watson sat again, then gestured to another cushion. I situated it closer to her—not too close—and made myself as comfortable as I could.

"It's all wars," she said.

"What?"

"It's all wars. Up here in your realm in the sky, it'll be nothing but wars, forever and ever."

"Is that what you want to talk about?" I asked.

"Isn't it what *you* want to talk about?"

"I'm here to talk with you, *about* you. Why start with *wars?"*

"It's true, isn't it? Thomas Avidità and the other Gods of the New Moons, they hate each other."

For the first time in my life, I experienced a *creeping feeling.* Dr. John Bell coined the term in 1815, in his *Principles of Surgery,* and only later in the writings of the romantics and gothics did it come to mean *dread.*

Gods of the New Moons, the same turn of phrase I'd used as a boy at a breakfast with Mr. Avidità. As far as I know, no one else had ever heard it.

Dread.

"Why do you call them that?" I asked. *"The Gods of the New Moons?"*

"That's what they are, aren't they?" She picked up one rose petal and tore it slowly into ribbons. "It's not as if anyone has successfully terraformed a planet, not like Mars or Venus is really *occupied.* Isn't that fair to say?"

"There're colonies," I said. "Science facilities."

"Colonies and science facilities don't amount to much— a few thousand people? That's not *new civilizations.*" She chuckled. "Yet the UPRC has got maybe thirty-million civilians in stations not so different from this one, or in converted asteroids like a bunch of shipwreck survivors crammed into life rafts. Thomas Avidità's got maybe *half* that. Who the fuck knows how many Nesteler's got? Might not be more than a few hundred, the goddamned-rich families of their executives *and that's it,* because Nesteler wouldn't give a shit if every other human in existence *ceased existing,* along with everything else that ever lived, so long as *they* get theirs."

"That last part might be true."

She retrieved another petal, tore it in half. For someone Mr. Avidità described as *gibbering* and *drooling,* Cassandra Watson seemed to have plenty to say, was plenty articulate.

"The Gods of the New Moons," she said, "because that's all they've got, their big claim to fame—a few dozen oversized space stations and some terraria, all orbiting *something* but not qualifying as much more than satellites. It's impressive, don't get me wrong, but really we're all sitting up here in flimsy-ass tin cans, hoping the UPRC or Nesteler or both don't attack us, send us careening back to Earth. Brimstone express, going down."

"You subscribe to the Law of Threes?" I asked.

"Exactly what I'm saying—*eagla*—that Avidità, Nesteler, and the UPRC will be up here fighting over the resources of System *forever.*"

"Grim." *Eagla?* What had *that* been?

"As grim as the fact that Nietzschean dominance competition between corporations is what caused the sixth great extinction—*uafásach*—and made Earth's surface so unstable as to make ongoing occupation *hellish?*"

Uafásach?

"Mr. Avidità," she said, "is a shit stain who was willing to rape and pillage Earth so as to stay competitive with other shit stains. He tells himself he isn't as bad as the other New Gods, that he cares more, that once he wins the war he'll make everything right, though Earthside he kept mining rare-earth minerals and selling consumerist shit nobody actually needed and developing weaponry for fighting his competition. Weaponry, I might add, which turned out *far* better at killing civilians than wiping out the heads of Nesteler or the UPRC's Party Leaders. Bás!"

This last word she barked, and I scooted from her. A dozen hidden cameras monitored this space, and orderlies and AIs waited to assist, though I wasn't too worried—Ms. Watson was human-standard, and on a good day I could bench press three hundred kilos.

"This is fascinating," I told her, "but I want to talk with you about your time with the Horned Lords, with their Queens, down in Alaska."

Now it was her turn to sit back, to scoot away. She fidgeted, biting the end of her thumb.

To herself she whispered, "Lies sleeping, lies dreaming, even death may die—"

"Ms. Watson, you were sent to infiltrate New Juneau, to gather information. What did you learn?"

Her gaze slid away and she wouldn't meet my eye. "Na damáistí," she said, "what happened is I learned the truth."

"What truth?"

"The New Gods are a bunch of petulant, egotistical children, and the Old Gods have taken notice. What a *mess* we've made."

"Mess?"

She wrung her hands and she screamed.

"What do you mean *Old Gods?*"

She lunged, planting one hand between us, shaking her fist at me. "I've *seen* them, you moron!"

"Seen what? Be specific. Our drones have spotted nothing—"

"The Old Gods *hate* your drones."

"—and we've certainly picked up no *Gods* on satellite—"

"But you have!"

"Explain."

"Twenty-one twenty-nine, October thirty-first, seventeen-twelve."

"What?"

"Fifty-eight degrees, twelve minutes, thirty-nine seconds north. One hundred thirty-four degrees, thirty-eight minutes, eighteen degrees west. Go look!"

"What'll I see?" I asked.

"Go look, godsdamn you!"

She leapt and knocked me onto my back. Before I could grab her wrists, she raked her fingernails across my face, gouging my cheek.

"Even death may die!" she keened. *"Even death may die!"*

A string of her drool puddled on my face. She babbled and tried to claw me again. Dr. Chowdhury flooded the room with gas, an anesthetic. Ms. Watson succumbed, collapsing upon me, her head against my chest.

After sucking in a breath, my vision narrowed and I too passed into unconsciousness.

THE NEXT DAY I checked the satellite archives.

2129.10.31.17:12. 58°12'39.3"N 134°38'18.8"W.

Most of the imagery of the Alaskan Panhandle showed me nothing but white. Infrared, ultraviolet, and radar tended towards blanks and interference. Yet one clear day in the waters west of Douglas Island and the fog-smeared city of New Juneau, *something* appeared in Young Bay. The AIs flagged it as a jellyfish bloom, possible but unlikely that far north, but to my eye it was clearly *not* a bloom.

Bigger than a blue whale, a mass surfaced for several seconds then submerged once more. Too amorphous for a whale; besides, blue whales were extinct. The phenomenon appeared in the archival data for twenty-two frames—then nothing.

Colossal. Organic.

What was it? Which corporation had engineered it?

I checked on Ms. Watson one more time. She lay on the floor of her cell, her arms bound, screaming incoherently in a language none of us recognized.

XVII. NEW JUNEAU

2131.4.12.20:33 PST
58°16'56.9"N 134°21'59.0"W
Alt 8m
Southeast Alaska (Dissolved)
New Juneau
6km to Destination

THE RAIN DRUMMED LONG into today but, by the time we walked the Thane Road to the ferry docks, the downpour had faded into mist. Now as I board the boat, the clouds fracture above the Gastineau Channel, the stars return, and the still-growing Moon frosts the sky.

The Horned Lord and I are the geriatric ferryman's only passengers, though the small boat couldn't carry more than a dozen anyway. Along the Gastineau, few lights cut the darkness, a handful of buildings on the mainland, but numerous docks house boats of nearly every kind, including larger ships. Lights glow from many.

Two *Cyclone V*-class U.S. Navy vessels, launched in the 2090s, anchor at a stout wharf. Beside them, too, float private yachts with military capabilities.

Fog clings to the mountainsides, but Mt. Roberts and Mt. Juneau glimmer, their snowy peaks reflecting the moonlight. These twin giants guard everything at their feet—the channel, the sea, the city. Most of New Juneau's population lives on Douglas Island's northeastern half. The island glitters with fallen constellations, the lights of three hundred thousand people, ten times the size Old Juneau before the inundations. A true city, and I'm sure there are more people living here than on what's left of Manhattan.

Outside northern China and the foothills of the Himalayas, this makes New Juneau one of the largest gatherings of humans on Earth.

As we cross the Channel, the sloshing waters reflect the city, as if we're entering two cities at once—a city material and a city spiritual—a surreality, a hermit queendom, home to *insular* folk. I don't know how many spies have entered New Juneau before me—dozens or hundreds—but I know of only one who has ever come out again. This isn't a place anyone enters, or departs, *lightly.*

In an echo of the Bonlin, bones both human and animal decorate the city's docks. Red and blue flags flutter from the tops of carved lodgepoles.

After the Lord and I disembark, he leads me uphill along a wide, straight avenue. Dense neighborhoods flank it, houses built beside winding alleys and paths, accreted as refugees arrived from across North America. Most of the buildings are, I note, timber or lumber. Near the lower washes, houses rest on stilts, and I recognize structures reinforced with steel cable. Good in earthquakes. Lighting varies from candles and hearths to high-performance, fractional-wattage LEDs, powered by hundreds of salvaged rooftop PV panels. PV coatings or tiles cover many south-facing surfaces. The city's technologies are a hodgepodge, probably recovered from as far south as half-drowned Seattle or as far east as burnt Edmonton.

Down here, a *lot* of technology has not survived into the twenty-second century.

The evening is late but not *so* late, and people walk the streets or sit on their porches. People of Asian descent, European descent, Native American descent, African Descent, and many twenty-first-century mixes of these. In a few appear oddities—eyes too large, noses flared in unusual ways, mouths too wide.

As the Horned Lord passes each and every person, they drop their gaze. Some kneel, calling to him, most in English but a few in French or Chinese.

"Hallowed," they say.

"A Reckoning," he answers.

Without fail, each man and woman watches me—curious, yes, some with eyes narrowed or widened—all with the low brow of mistrust. Several hurry indoors or down side streets.

A second Horned Lord meets my guide and they exchange a few sentences.

Of the languages still spoken by humanity, I know at least a smattering of most. Yet I do not recognize the tongue which they speak and this fact, more than walls of bone or unexplained biota, unnerves me.

"Come on," my guide says to me, and with his new companion we continue.

Several hundred meters up, the street empties onto a hilltop where a long building occupies the center of a cobblestone square. The building's gable reaches twelve meters above ground, its roof reminding me of an ancient wooden longship turned upside down, darkened by planks greening with moss. Truss ends project from the tops of the walls, timber carved to resemble dragons' heads. Under the eaves, two levels of slender windows punctuate the building's long sides. Firelight flickers from within, and aromatic smoke rises from two expansive stone chimneys. The building's three-meter-high doors are closed, their carven surfaces depicting myriad animals in a sylvan idyll.

Inside, a man sings. In French, sounds like.

Voices drift across the square.

The two Horned Lords flank me. Several more approach, their hewing spears in hand. Crowds gather behind the Lords, *hundreds* shuffling up every street, craning their necks to see me.

I am fucked.

Turning to my guide I say, "I never caught your name?"

"I am the Horned Lord," he says, the corners of his stained mouth curling.

His companion says, "And I am the Horned Lord."

Two others take up positions behind me.

"I am the Horned Lord," says the third.

The fourth says, "I am the Horned Lord."

They *are* different men. Different heights, different colors, different bodies. The tonalities of their voices differ, too, but their inflections and accents—identical.

"I am the Horned Lord," says a fifth. "Now kneel."

A spear haft strikes the back of my knees and I drop. The pain rattles up my hips, into my spine. In reflex I keep my left arm around the baby.

"Crawl," says the Horned Lord—it doesn't matter which one.

"What?"

"Crawl."

The slender edge of a spearpoint lies against the back of my neck, nicks my skin, lets me know how sharp it is.

My left arm remains fixed, carrying the baby's weight, and his shrill cry reverberates. The crowd remains silent. On my knees, only my right hand keeping me stable, I shuffle forward. The Horned Lords herd me toward the building and, still crawling, I ascend its steps. The wooden doors swing outward, slabs thick as my body and reinforced in bronze.

Light spills across me, bringing with it an aroma of roasted meats and vegetables. The singing grows louder.

The building is tripartite—a central hall reaches to the gable, between double-storied volumes to either side, not arcades as in a christian church but semi-private bowers, sleeping nooks reached by ladders. Long tables parallel a common space, with a slender, copper-hooded hearth at its center. At the hall's end rises a dais with two thrones, a smaller hearth behind them.

Many dozens of people occupy the hall, some peering from the bowers, others gathered at the tables. Standing on a bench, the singer continues:

> *"Maintes et maintes fois, de mauvaises choses*
> *m'ont attaqué,*
> *caché et chassé, mais je suis devenu fou,*
> *frapper aussi fort que possible avec mon épée,*
> *ma chair n'était pas pour le festin."*

Strange to hear *Beowulf* in French. But why not? The flat of the spearpoint smacks the backs of my thighs, drives me past the central hearth. When I reach the foot of the dais, I raise my head, my attention drawn to the thrones.

I humble myself before the Queens.

XVIII. SUFFICIENTLY ADVANCED

Recollected
2131.3.11.7:20 GMT
Alt 40.2E6m
High Earth Orbit
EIK-Cel Station

S ECOND-TO-LAST TIME I saw Mr. Avidità, before my launch into space with the baby-who-would-be-Alastar, the King and I sparred in his private dojo. We traded kicks and punches, breathless, between snippets of conversation.

"I *cannot* stress enough," he said, "you have only *four* objectives."

I attempted to sweep his feet, but he leapt away. He landed too hard on his heel, off balance, and I managed to graze his ribs. Springing back from a sidekick, I centered myself and reassessed my strategy.

"I was going to ask you about the objectives, Your Grace."

"Oh?"

He flew at me, a volley of kicks, then tried to leverage me against his hip, to slam me to the mats. I rolled across his back and punched his kidney. Grunting, he spun away, clenching his teeth.

"The first is clear enough," I said. "Deliver the baby to New Juneau."

"As far as we can tell, young children are welcome there, all adopted. It's about as safe a place on Earth a child could be."

"Excepting an Avidità facility?"

He steadied his breath. "Naturally."

Mr. Avidità lunged, jabs and uppercuts, street-fighter style. Weaving, I locked my leg behind his and slammed him to the mat. Before I could pin him, he rolled and kipped to his feet.

"I'm a fan of the fourth objective," I said.

He laughed. "I'd appreciate it if you could pull that one off too."

Number four required I survive, return to San Francisco, and debrief. Harques are rare amongst Avidità Corporation's crèche products, and we represent significant investments. Our transhuman talents require no implants or digital technologies and, on occasion, this makes us excellent spies.

But we have to survive in order to report.

"Objectives two and three, though, they confuse me," I admitted.

"Good thing we made time for this review."

We fell into loose sparring, ritualized kickboxing—wet slaps of salty flesh, our labored breathing, the shuffle of feet.

"Secondary to installing the infant into their midst, Aur, I'd need to know what's happening on Wrangell Island. It's the locus of the phenomenon."

A punch, a kick. Slower attacks.

"What about objective three?" I asked.

"I doubt you'll get the chance."

"If I do?"

"I leave it up to your judgment, Aur." His jab clipped my right cheek.

Regaining my balance, I said, "I'm not sure I trust my judgment."

Quick punches, one-two, one-two. Mr. Avidità forced me back on my heels.

"You remember the day you got Flapjacks?" he asked.

Silly question.

The bunny. The airlock.

"That day," he said, "you showed me everything I needed to know about you. I trust you, when your time comes again, to choose right."

I threw everything at him—kicks, punches, knees, elbows, locks, trips, throws. I landed cursory blows, drove him to the edge of the tatamis.

The mats tilted upward and smacked me in the face. Locking my shoulder, Mr. Avidità pressed my cheek into the floor.

"I trust your judgment," he said, his breath hot against my ear, vibrating with an intimacy so common between fighting men. "You aren't, however, the *best* warrior we've ever trained."

"Never claimed to be, Your Grace."

"Whether you kill Bett or Cailín, you decide. After all, *I* didn't pull the trigger, not when I had a chance, not when I could've blown them from the water."

"I've watched the holovids. I'm curious—why *didn't* you?"

"Curiosity." He let me up and we stood together, panting, catching our breath. "I'm still eighty-percent convinced," he said, "whatever's going on in their so-called kingdom—queendom?—is a secret project, one of our competitor's skunkworks. If that's the case, Aur, then the Queens need to die."

"And if it's not?"

"We'll reassess. *Curiosity.*"

Closing out the session, we bowed, offering each other respect not as father and son, or creator and created, but as momentary equals. He clasped my shoulder.

"Remember, Aur, whatever's going on in Alaska and the Yukon, there's a rational, technical, scientific explanation. Cailín Byrne was a biotech executive from Dublin. Bett Ukweli was a going-nowhere, working-class woman from Winnipeg. Now they're Queens, priestesses, practically worshipped as Goddesses—the center of a cult. *Only* a cult, a curtain of superstition behind smoke and mirrors. The most valuable thing you can do is find the curtain, pull it back, and show me the wizard."

I wiped the sweat from my forehead, downed a bottle of water, and managed a laugh. "What if it's wizards all the way down?" I asked, paraphrasing Stephen Hawking paraphrasing Bertrand Russell.

With a half shrug he said, "Any con-job sufficiently advanced—"

"I understand," I replied. "Cults, smoke and mirrors, curtains. I'll survive, Mr. Avidità, and I'll come back."

He put his arm around my shoulder and, together, we walked to the showers.

XIX. LAMINATE THRONES

2131.4.12.21:26 PST
58°15'52.8"N 134°28'24.3"W
Alt 630m
Southeast Alaska (Dissolved)
New Juneau
Hall of the Queens
0km to Destination

THE HORNED LORD WHO was my guide these last few days, he sets down his heavy backpack, retrieves from it my Walther pistol, and chambers a round. Foolish of me to think he hadn't taken it from Garth. The gun's muzzle presses to the back of my skull.

I cradle the baby and he's screaming at the top of his tiny, powerful, endlessly expressive lungs. Wood fires crackle in the hearths, scenting the hall with cedar and pinewood. Other odors provide undertones—human musk, honeyed liquor, hemp, something else earthy and unfamiliar. The singer has paused his *Beowulf* and no one speaks.

I split my attention between studying the Queens and estimating my odds at rolling aside before the Lord pulls the trigger. A poor bet, but greater than zero.

From my place on the floor I'm closest to Queen Cailín. The Irishwoman's azure dress covers her to her ankles, and she presses her bare feet against the floor. Those ankles are milky pale, her shoulders as fair but peppered in freckles. Her limbs, her toes, her fingers, her slender collarbones, their length makes me think of the fossils of an archaeopteryx or pterodactyl; her dark hair, of the earth in which those bones might lie. A scar above her clavicle tells the story of an old gunshot wound, one which could have been fatal. Her eyes, as I expected from her photographs, are absurdly blue.

An old dog lies on the floor between her and her wife.

Queen Bettina lounges sideways across her throne, her elbows propped on one of its arms, her knees draped across the other. Also barefoot, she wears deerskin leggings and a long blouse. Her hair surrounds her head in a wild, dark corona. In the firelight her brown eyes sparkle into a peculiar amber.

No crowns adorn the Queens' heads.

I cannot help but note the color of their lips, their deep, strangely calming, coal-violet. The shade differs from the mouths of the Horned Lords, which is lighter, redder, angrier.

Cailín leans forward. "You're name is Aur?"

"It is, Highness."

Bettina's laugh is genial, no derision, no judgment. "None of that here, Aur. No *Your Majesties*. No *Your Highnesses.*"

"How should I address you?"

"As Bettina," says Bettina.

"As Cailín," says Cailín.

"You're the Queens of the Horned Lord," I say.

"And this is the Hall of the Queens," Bettina says, "but let's not grovel or rest on ceremony, not now."

A fluttering of wings and feathers passes through the hall, and the raven called Nevermore lands on the back of Bettina's throne. He's gigantic, flexing his wings and preening. Bettina lifts her hand, slides her fingers through the soft plumage of his ruff.

The raven caws, fiercely loud in the confines. The baby hiccoughs, blows snot, and quiets to a murmur.

The gun still presses the back of my head. Another Horned Lord brings his spearhead to my throat, its flat against my larynx. If he slits my throat, the baby will be showering in my blood.

"Where did you come from, Aur?" asks Bettina.

I tell them the story of the woman, her son, the bandits, the farm, the baby. As practiced as before, I miss no details.

"We found her farm," says Cailín, "the turned fields, the bodies, the woman and her son right where you say you buried them."

What they found doesn't surprise me. I wonder who the dead woman and dead boy had been? I wonder about the four so-called bandits? Mr. Avidità would not have missed any details either, would have ensured my lies look like truths under scrutiny. What *does* surprise me is that the Queens could have already verified the site, could already know my story, could have sent anyone to investigate and already received word back. This land is big and few can move as speedily as I have. Vehicles could have crossed that ground no quicker, at no time have I seen planes or helicopters, and these people do not seem to employ drones.

More importantly, Avidità intelligence has reported little radio chatter around the Faen and, to our knowledge, no quantum telecommunications. From our own measurements, we know wireless technologies don't work well here, not within a three-hundred-kilometer radius. We must have missed something?

I wait for Cailín to continue.

"This is the woman's babe," she says, "at your chest?"

"Yes."

"You've brought him to place into our safekeeping?"

"Yes," I say, almost adding *Your Grace.*

"What's the child's name?" she asks.

"I don't know."

"You stayed with the woman, yet you don't know?"

"I was only at her farm a few days," I explain. "Her name was Stephanie but, honestly, the kids' names slipped right the fuck out my brain."

It's an ironic lie, a clever one, for a Harque.

Cailín says, "We'll name him Alastar."

"Let Aur sit up," Bettina says to the Horned Lords.

They do, but the pistol remains at my head.

Cailín gestures toward a bower, to a woman reclining in it. The woman's sleeping space is decorated in French toile canvas and linen—as unique as every other bower. At least some of the time, many people *live* here, customize their corners of it, make it their own. This isn't a court reserved for official proceedings, I realize, but an extended domestic arrangement. The dozens of witnesses here, they are the Queens' adopted family.

This woman slides from her bed. She wraps a robe around herself, comes forward, and stretches her arms toward me. Sympathetic eyes, short hair the color of dry savanna grasses, a soft roundness to her which belies a fortitude, something I intuit more than observe.

I unstrap the baby, who fusses and squirms, and hand him up to her. He leaves my possession, no longer my responsibility, the first of my mission's objectives discharged. The woman retreats with him to her bower.

"Who do you serve?" Bettina asks.

Sitting back on my heels, I push against the muzzle at my skull.

"It's all right," says Cailín. "You can tell us."

"I've made it on my own out there," I say, "for years. I don't serve anyone but myself."

"Why make your way west now?"

"I'm tired of making it on my own."

"Anyone can understand that," the Irishwoman says, her brogue charming. "Whoever wants to be alone?"

"You haven't been out there for *years,*" says Bettina. "You haven't been out there a *month.*"

Pressing my tongue to the roof of my mouth, I prepare my retort. "I—"

"Oh, stop it," she says, the hint of a laugh in her words. "Tell us the truth, Aur, or we'll find out whether one Horned Lord can slit your throat faster than the other one can blow your brains out."

They know.

"I serve Thomas Avidità," I say.

Bettina claps once. "Was that so difficult?"

"How did you—?"

"We weren't certain," she says, "but we knew you were lying."

"How?"

"Like magicians, we've no obligation to reveal our secrets."

"Fair."

"Let me guess," says Bettina, "Avidità dropped you somewhere in the Yukon, let you look like you've dragged yourself a few hundred kilometers?"

"Yes."

"You happen across the mother's homestead, see she's preparing a spring sowing, maybe feel sorry for her two children?" Bettina swivels, more dignified in her throne, a chair striated in degrees of white which contrast her brown skin.

"It slows you down, but you've actually got a heart and you agree to stay awhile."

"Yes," I say.

The raven caws, almost a cackle, then hops to Cailín's throne.

"The bandits," Cailín says, "they must've surprised you."

"Why do you say that?" I ask.

"You're a black-ops soldier sent by the most powerful man in System. They were four desperate ruffians armed with second-rate guns and homemade ammunition."

"You're not wrong."

"The best plans cannot account for every variable."

"Admirable," says Bettina, "saving the baby."

"I'm not a monster," I say.

"That remains to be seen."

Bettina stands, her movements fluid. She's short, about 163cm and stockier than her wife, but her presence fills the room.

"Give him his gun," she tells the Horned Lord behind me.

My heart pumps a half dozen times before the muzzle pulls away. The Horned Lord holds the pistol, handle first, over my shoulder, but the second Lord keeps his spear at my neck.

I wish my pack weren't strapped to my shoulder. It's still heavy, will slow me, but I make my choice.

Bypassing the gun, I grab the spear haft, break it, and hit its wielder under the jaw. The blow lifts the man, tosses him, and splinters fly. The motion brings me to my feet and, as I'd hoped, the man behind me stood near enough that my pack knocks him off balance. Whatever the Horned Lords are now, they were born human-standard, and in taking the Walther from him I snap his wrist.

By weight I assess my Walther—fully loaded—and I put one bullet each into the Lords nearest me, into the meat of their thighs, careful to miss arteries. The shots exact gasps and screams from onlookers. Three more Horned Lords attack. Dodging a thrown spear, I fire three more times, and the men stumble or fall.

In the peculiar detail-rich perception of combat, I absorb the men's expressions, not an ounce of pain in them or, more accurately, they dismiss their pain. They limp or crawl toward me, but I have at least earned a buffer.

I swivel.

Bettina Ukweli stands close enough for me to discern the hazel in her irises. My gun sights aline for the center of her forehead, but something about her reminds me of Imka.

Poor Imka.

Why would I think of her *now?*

Have you ever experienced night terrors? You so desperately wish to move, to thrash about, to fight. Nothing whatsoever holds you except the sheets of your bed, but there you are, as if clasped in chains.

I cannot make myself squeeze the trigger.

"I'd hoped something better from you," Bettina says. The dog barks. Where has the raven gone? "The world is brutish," she adds, "but does that mean we've *all* got to be brutes?"

The room darkens and shadows arise behind me. Several men and women *prostrate* themselves, and not for the Queens. Something hard strikes the back of my head, my occipital lobe, and I crumple onto the flagstones at Bettina's feet. The gun bounces from me and spins across the floor.

"Put him with the other offerings," says Cailín, sounding distraught, "and get the injured to Dr. Falwell."

My vision tunnels and, for whatever reason, I focus on Bettina's empty throne. It's devotedly crafted from spliced bones—animal, human, hundreds of fragments. Some master builder had laminated them, planed them, and polished them, as if Charles Rennie Mackintosh had returned from the dead to design the chairs of barbarian royalty.

"Other *offerings?*" I ask.

The second blow lands behind my right ear—

XX. SACRIFICES
[OR, INTELLIGENCE, PART II]

Unknown Time
Unknown Location
Alt 2m

THE BACK OF MY head hurts like a motherfucker. My sense of geography is like a century-old, crushed aluminum can; my sense of time, like the soda label once printed on it. You know the kind—until a few decades ago, Avidità Corporation was still mining them from landfills. I blink into a flat, gray sky. Seaspray tickles my nose, the odor of brine, and the rolling crash of waves and an incoming tide snaps me into consciousness.

I'm in a *lot* of trouble.

Knotted ropes scratch my wrists. My toes are numb, and I wonder how long I've been standing barefoot on this platform, how many of its splinters are buried in my skin.

It'll take awhile to recalibrate my position and timestamp. Early morning, I estimate, not quite sunrise and I doubt I've been unconscious even nine hours. I've got a concussion but I don't think it's too serious. To my periphery extend dense pine forests, up and down the waterline, rising to an island peak behind me.

Douglas Island? Probably?

Someone is moaning in Chinese. Hard to focus on it, my head throbs.

I could say I'm on a *beach,* but that isn't right. There're few oceanside beaches anywhere in the world. Most have been wiped away, are sixty meters down, will reform only after centuries or millennia of tidal scouring. This isn't a beach, only a stretch where granite and alkali soils meet the sea.

The ropes bind me to a post, a tree trunk stripped of bark and branches. Three or four meters beneath the platform, a field of seaweed-draped stumps reaches into the lashing waves. To my right, five more elevated platforms line this rocky verge, complete with five more tied victims. Five Chinese, not American born but obvious DPRC. One is carping on and on, and now my brain translates:

"What have I done for this?" he cries. "Madam President, is there no hope? What will happen?!" He mutters, something quick, idiomatic, then he adds, "Please, Madam President, let me die without pain—"

Prattling idiot.

I'm struck by how he's speaking to the Party Leader, who almost certainly cannot hear him and who most definitely cannot help him. He's talking to himself really, projecting, entreating a mortal leader he's always thought omnipotent.

His four compatriots, two men and two women, wait in silence for whatever's coming. All six of us face the sea, and behind us several ravens caw and chatter.

Cailín Byrne's voice: "Ph'nglui mglw'nafh Cthulhu R'lyeh wgah'nagl fhtagn."

The words from my dream, spoken not by the boy but by her. I'm not sure where she's standing, can't turn my head far enough. The world shifts a degree, a lurch of vertigo, and I'm scouring my memory for where I might've heard those words before her, before the dream, some other waking memory. None.

Their identicalness is impossible. Yet—

"Intinn Domhain," she says, "take these sacrifices, our offering of good will."

The last eight words, though, I understood. I test my bindings, cannot help but notice my rope is thicker, stronger than that which binds the DPRC nationals.

Fog slithers across the choppy, white-capped, sharp waters, veiling other tree-covered islands, their shapes indistinct. Surf licks the posts and gusts fling the water to dapple my face. The sky lightens, the sunrise behind me, blocked by the island.

Cailín continues to speak, but her language shifts, the same tongue spoken by the Horned Lords after my arrival in New Juneau. The intensity of her words rises, almost a song, and other voices adopt the melody. A chorus.

How many people are behind me?!

Their chorus ends, "—a Reckoning."

A dozen meters beyond shore, the sea froths and bubbles. The churning water brightens from slate gray to mesmerizing hues of green and purple. It develops a gargantuan back, a spiny dome swelling, and the displaced waters roar.

Bursting from the tidal waves, an elongated mass wraps itself around the closest UPRC man and, as quickly, it returns to the sea. The man is gone, along with the platform he stood on and most of the post which held it.

I try breaking my bonds, straining until the hemp cuts my skin. I might be crying out, might be screaming *what the fuck, what the fuck,* but my body keeps moving, keeps fighting. My wrists are bleeding.

The sea erupts with powerful, leathery, acrid flesh. Protuberances, pseudopods, amorphous limbs.

The DPRC sad-sacks are screaming their lungs out, all but one, an old man who's a better stoic than I am.

Crack!

His entire post vanishes and he with it, whipped into the sea. Another log-sized appendage slaps one of the women, sticks to her, slimes her. Her shriek pains my ears. She *burns,* the slime caustic and heinous, then she's torn from her platform. Her bloodied right arm dangles from its bonds.

Crack!

Crack!

Down to me. The ocean convulses, bursts with pseudopods, growths of leather and muscle large around as hippos. Their tips curl near my face. One flares, unrolling tentacles from tentacles, and a dozen tiny eyes open along each. A reek of ammonia and mucus forces a gag from my throat.

Sapient.

Thick with palpable intelligence, the air chokes me, infiltrates me, makes me feel as if my brain is outgrowing my skull, like meningitis, like the promise of death.

And *age.*

Such age! Timeless, it's so old that Mr. Avidità's lifespan is nothing to it. The ages of Biblical patriarchs, nothing. Old when the Roman Empire—the meningitis of Europe—outgrew its bounds. Old when the Egyptians constructed their pyramids. Old when humans built the first cities. Old when hominids still hunted mammoths. Old when apes climbed from the trees to wander the grasslands. Old now when humanity out-swells the Solar System—the meningitis of the Milky Way.

Guzzling up all the milk Hera has to give, drinking her dry, leaving nothing.

Sapience.

So much more intelligent than I, the Thing in the Water hates me the way a buffalo hates flies. I'm nothing to it, yet, yet—

Curiosity.

Its pseudopods flare, like nostrils taking in a outsized breath. Membranes open. A hundred beady, black, shark-like pupils consider me.

Then retreat into the sea, extensions withdrawn, the mass settling into the waves, submerging, quieting, deepening, stilling. Gone. The waves lap as before and the breeze persists as before, save warmer and somehow sweeter.

"Cut the spaceman down," says Cailín, "help him walk."

I'm whispering, "Thank you, thank you," though to whom I'm not sure, and I'm sure no one can hear me. "Thank you, thank you."

"If he causes any trouble though," comes her Irish lilt, "don't hesitate to put a shotgun to his head and pull the trigger."

XXI. VICTORIES ARE TEMPORARY

Recollected
2119.9.9.4:11 GMT
1.26au from Sol
Nesteler Martian Window 42
Operation Barrel Fish

O VER THE YEARS I tried to forget the killings I made in Avidità Corporation's name, but a Harque seldom forgets. I've tried not to think of them as *murders,* too, but the more I pondered them, the more murderous they've felt. After the Battle at Africa IV, I participated in seven off-Station combat missions between the orbits of Earth and Jupiter. These racked up more than seventy-eight confirmed kills.

Not as skilled a murder-squad soldier as my brothers, but no slouch either.

As I've aged, the more ridiculous it seems that my life should account for seventy-eight others. Eighty-three since my arrival to Earth, including the poor bastard on the stake.

In the heyday of Mars's colonization, a hundred nation states and corporations divided the Red Planet. Nesteler Group made the biggest initial investment, and it engineered the re-firing of Mars's iron core. The spin-up took twenty-seven years, during which Nesteler intimidated, sued, or outright slaughtered every other competitor for Martian territory. As of 2119, there were eight hundred eighty-four Martian colonies— only industrial or scientific operations remained—but in fact eight hundred eighty-two had become either vendors to or wholly owned subsidiaries of Nesteler Group. The remaining two were South Pole operations of the UPRC.

Mars itself became unassailable Nesteler territory. Its supply lines, though—

In the intervening years, Nesteler established regular shipment windows between Mars, its Earthbound Stations, and its other operations around System. *Operation Barrel Fish* required ninety-two Avidità bombers and strikers on a stealth run to intercept Nesteler's *Window 42*. Forty-four ships from the UPRC joined us, because in unending warfare the enemy of my enemy *is* my enemy but sometimes we join forces anyway because on that particular day the third party frightens the shit out of us.

In the final approach we ran silent, every ship powered down. Operating this way, ships bleed heat and crews can freeze to death long before they pollute their air with carbon dioxide. Yet running dark minimized the chances the Nesteler caravan would detect us.

Zeroing on Nesteler's active pings—stealth was not their strategy—we allowed Newton's first law to do its magic, carrying us in a precise arc defined by the gravitational tug of Sol, moving at 3600km per second. The trajectory brought us across the caravan at a comparative speed of 780km per hour— so slow our systems could power up, target every Nesteler vessel, and strike.

The caravan contained a mix of defenders and transports. Nesteler depended on AIs and robotics—there'd be few humans on their ships. Like most strikes in space, this one happened in a blink, no dogfighting, no rerouting, no second chances. Post-strike, our active pings reported a ninety-one percent destroy rate. In four seconds, Nesteler fired more than three hundred missiles and eight thousand laser pulses. Twenty percent of Avidità's ships ceased to exist, evaporated. The UPRC's losses were similar—

Until Avidità's second strike intercepted us, annihilating every remaining UPRC vessel. We lost only seven more. Once I'd returned to Station, Mr. Avidità explained the deceit to me:

"Between us, the UPRC, and Nesteler," he said, "there can exist no such concepts as *truth* or *lies*. We *know* we're lying to each other. So instead our calculations depend on *what the lie happens to be this time* and *how confident we are that our lie is more convincing than theirs*. Next time, perhaps, we'll side with Nesteler against the UPRC, and perhaps Nesteler will guess better than we and our side will suffer the devastating losses. When *we* gain too much power, we'll find the UPRC will side with Nesteler against us. This pattern will continue ad infinitum."

"Isn't that terribly wasteful?" I asked, enjoying the view of his botanical gardens, grateful for a cup of tea. "Wouldn't it be better if the UPRC, Nesteler, and Avidità brokered a peace and worked together to create the best System they possibly could?"

"You're right," he said. "It *would* be best, but it'll never be, so we're stuck in a classic prisoner's dilemma, filled with mistrust, always fighting for dominance."

"Why? Why *can't* there be peace? Surely it's the most rational desire, the only one which guarantees a continued existence for all sides."

He refilled my teacup. "I don't believe peace is possible. Do you follow me? I lead Avidità Corporation. It exists and does what it does at *my* pleasure, and *I do not believe peace is possible*. Therefore Avidità will *never* lower its guard, will *never* stop seeking supremacy over its enemies, no matter how unlikely we'll obtain such supremacy."

Was the tea bitter, over-steeped? "I understand, Your Grace."

"Here's how it is—the UPRC doesn't believe it either, and their Party Leaders are a bunch of bigoted pricks anyway."

He didn't need to remind me about Nesteler. Over the years the Nesteler Oligarchy had made its attitudes clear. In its eyes, everyone outside Nesteler's stock-holding families were *surplus population*. The UPRC gave citizenship only to those who could trace their lineage to Yuan-dynasty China.

"I could force myself," said Mr. Avidità. "I could wake tomorrow and tell myself, 'It's the right thing to do, to give peace a chance, Lennon style. We'll turn the other cheek. We'll take the high road. Today,' I could declare, 'the dove of peace will fly, and we'll make the first overtures to stop the violence.'"

Mr. Avidità used clichés as weapons of disdain.

"What would happen then?" I asked.

He stared at the tablecloth, at the tea service, at the empty plates. His fingertips traipsed along the china teapot, played with the lid, wrapped around the handle. He flung it at the nearest wall and it shattered into countless, tiny, glittering ceramic fragments. The remaining tea splashed across a fortune in gold-woven wallpaper.

"We wouldn't last long," he said, "and the UPRC and Nesteler would divide our carcass between them."

I was pretty sure I agreed. I'm pretty sure I agree now.

"Don't forget this, Aur." He fixed me with his gaze, that peculiar shade of green and gray in his irises. "All victories are only temporary—until your enemies cease to exist."

XXIII. REPRIEVE

2131.4.13.14:53 PST
58°15'52.8"N 134°28'24.3"W
Alt 630m
The Faen
New Juneau
Hall of the Queens

COMFORT, SOFTNESS, WARMTH. Mainly from the woman cuddled against me.

A fading ache at the back of my head. Irritation along the soles of my feet.

I'm naked. So is she.

Luxurious sheets enfold us and I remember I'm lying in a bower inside the Hall of the Queens. The climb from Douglas Island's northwest shore had followed a meticulously laid flagstone stair edged with springtime grasses, budding flowers, and skulls. I'd walked on my own, then leaned on the shoulders of the celebrants who'd come to witness my death. Finally, they'd carried me after my bleeding feet failed.

Now, the woman presses against my back, stretches, and arcs with the feline happiness of a satisfying nap. About my age, relaxed, trusting, round, beautiful—mousy-brown hair, skin fair and soft as whipped cream. Her brown eyes blink, focus, and take me in.

"You need to bathe," she says.

"Agreed," I reply.

"At least you're not cold anymore."

"Early springtime seas? This close to the arctic circle? Lashed to a goddamned pole? Goddamn, yes, I was cold."

Her legs, hooked over mine, tug me against her. "Hypothermia and shock can kill."

I'm probably tougher than she believes. "You've got *that* right."

She snuggles, as if we were lovers, as if I knew what the hell her name was.

"Where am I?" I ask.

"In the Hall of the Queens."

"I understand, but where *am* I?"

"In my bed."

"Whose bed?"

"I'm Ruby."

"I'm Aur."

"I know."

"*Why* am I in your bed?"

She rolls her eyes.

"This is a thing? You bring cold men into your bed?"

"Today I did." She tugs the blankets around us. "I could have let you freeze."

"Don't get me wrong," I say. "I'm grateful."

She snorts softly, dismissively. "In the future, maybe I'll keep my bed to myself."

On any other day, in any other circumstances, I'd stop asking questions and nestle in. She's soft and curvaceous and smells like lavender.

Also, I've never been this close to an undressed woman before.

"This morning," I say, "what the fuck happ—"

She presses her fingertip to my lips. "Shh."

This morning, I think, *I was lashed to splintered wood and offered up to a—*

A what?

Its presence echoes. *Cthulhu fhtagn.* The words won't leave me alone.

"You're safe," she says.

No such thing as safety, said the Horned Lord.

Curtains enclose the bower, but the narrow parting between them frames a portion of the Hall of the Queens, including a length of the central hearth. Daylight streams from clerestory windows, bathing the flagstones in gold. Other voices, eight which I can discern, talk about nothing I care about. Fishing, farming, changes in weather. Someone laughs. Sounds of intimate conversation—friends or lovers chatting.

"Why am I still alive?" I ask.

"The Old One didn't want you," says Ruby.

Old One.

"Even if I survived that," I say, "the spies of competing powers are usually imprisoned, questioned, tortured, and eventually either exchanged as leverage or executed. They're not cuddled in bed to save them from hypothermia."

She rolls onto her side, leaning on her elbow and propping her head against her hand. "I don't know much about *spies* or what *powers* do with them."

A faint stain colors her lips, not makeup but a rosy, pink-petal discoloration of the flesh.

"What is it you do here, Ruby?"

She opens her mouth to answer but, before she can, Bettina's voice fills the hall: "She serves me, Aur."

I sit, bunching the sheets around my waist. Ruby stretches, shakes off her nap-time languor, and still naked she climbs from the bed. Her breasts sway, pendulous and hypnotic, before she sweeps aside the curtains and descends a ladder to the floor. Around the hall are a dozen other members of the Queens' retinue, relaxing but also keeping half an eye on me. Near the laminate thrones, three Horned Lords stand guard.

Bettina walks toward me, passing between the thrones. The old dog accompanies her.

"Don't suppose," I say, "you've got my clothes?"

Ruby meets Bettina, kisses her, then saunters by the smaller hearth to a heavy door. Once she's gone through it, the door closes, the sound reverberating.

"We burned them," Bettina says.

"It's a little cold outside," I say, "don't you think?"

She shrugs. "You'd be surprised. Some of New Juneau's residents *bathe* in ice water."

"Not your thing?"

"No!" She laughs. "Gods, no. I'm embarrassed to say so, but I hate being cold, despise cold weather. Before Blight, living in Winnipeg, I loathed wintertime."

"I don't blame you."

"When I was still living with my parents," she said, "I had a poster of Costa Rica on my bedroom wall, some idyllic beach, tropical trees."

"Underwater now."

She nodded. "I'll have some clothes brought to you. Then I'd like you to meet me in the Square."

"All right."

"Though you must promise me something."

"What?"

"No more assassination attempts."

I cannot help but smile. "All right."

§

TWO YOUNG MEN BRING me to a tub of hot water. They provide soap and sponges, and I scrub myself until I'm fresh as a soaped-down newborn calf. Simple leather shoes, a tunic, and pants of finely spun alpaca, the clothes Bettina provided me took skill to make but, to be honest, they itch. They're loose, too, something of a trash-bag fit. The young men also give me a fleece coat, too hot for afternoon sunlight, but I sling it over my shoulder.

I step through the hall's front doors and find a city alive. Tents and booths cram the hilltop plaza which was, last night, empty. Hundreds of people crowd the aisles, trading dozens of kinds of wares. Nowhere does anyone exchange money, physically or digitally, but a marketplace exists here, one whose rules of commerce I don't understand.

Children play. One girl hides behind the legs of her mother, then leaps at a small boy, giggling and chasing. There're children, I realize, who've lived in New Juneau their entire lives. This *is* their normal, the only reality they've ever experienced.

The adults, more serious, bear the signs of long-suffered trauma, hyper-aware, untrusting. PTSD. Yet they too chatter, laugh, share. What the Queens have built here, it's better than whatever came before it, safer for these people than anywhere since Blight or in the years after the Third Pulse, during the economic collapses, the riots, the food shortages.

As Bettina approaches me, accompanied by two Horned Lords, everyone in their path bows or kneels.

The Queen tugs a bearskin cloak around herself. "Can your feet handle a hike?" she asks me.

"I can manage."

"Good. I want to show you something."

For less than a klick, Bettina, the Lords, and I walk west through the winding, bustling, crowded streets. As always the Lords have their spears. Unarmed, Bettina carries only a backpack across her shoulder.

Along the way I note stormwater grates, signs of a sewage system, and water pipes. From wells? An aqueduct or pipeline from the mainland? At the city's far edge, a timber wall divides the streets from the forest. For a moment I fear we're returning to the sacrificial clearing, that at the shore Bettina will offer me up once more, but instead we follow a different path, taking us southwest. We return to the waterline, yes, but this time to a wharf.

"Where're we going?" I ask.

"A graveyard."

Hard for me to imagine a real graveyard. On Station, by comparison, we compost the dead.

The four of us board a boat and the Horned Lords row us south, toward a promontory on Admiralty Island. They're strong, tireless, and grim. The waters slosh, the air once more near freezing, and now I wrap myself in the fleece coat.

"You must be hungry?" Bettina asks me.

"I am."

"Ask for food."

"What?"

"Ask me for food," she says.

Sitting at the transom, I'm the only one of the four of us who watches where we're going. The Horned Lords, at the rowing benches, look back at me, their expressions hard. Bettina sits across from me, close enough I could strike her.

But I promised.

"All right," I say, "may I have some food?"

She unslings her backpack. "What did you see this morning?"

"A monster."

"What kind of monster?"

Terrifying? Horrific? Pestilential?

Then I realize, "An *old* monster."

"Good." She pulls a smaller bag from her backpack and unties it. The aroma of fresh meat and vegetables mixes with brine. "What does that tell you, Aur?"

I *am* hungry. "It tells me—"

"It's hard to say it, right? Go ahead, say it."

"It tells me, whatever the monster was, it's not something made by the UPRC, not produced by Nesteler, not bred by any industry."

"What does that *mean?*"

"I—I don't know what the fuck it means."

She smiles and, even more than last night, she reminds me of Imka. Before leaving EIK-Cel I had, of course, studied dozens of images of Bettina Ukweli. Her hair has grown wilder, and now she wears woven clothes and leathers and furs instead of secondhand clothes bought in the San Francisco markets, but she hasn't aged a day. She unpacks a wooden bowl and a hand-forged fork, then fills the bowl with chunks of tender chicken and sautéed root vegetables.

It's delicious, the Grist of the Gods, savory and fresh. I wolf down a few mouthfuls.

"It means," she says, "everything you know is wrong. *Everything.*"

"Do you worship that—that thing?"

She laughs. "Hell, no! *Those* slimy motherfuckers?"

"What, then, what was all that about, the offering, the sacrificing? Those Chinese, it took them all, they're *dead.*"

"We supplicate the Spawn, the Deep Ones, the Gods of the Horizon—children of Dagon. Our pacts with them are critical for our future."

"I don't understand."

With a few more greedy bites, I empty the bowl. Bettina takes it from me, refills it, and hands it back. Simple food, yes, but some of the best I've ever tasted.

"It's nothing I can explain so simply," she says. "That'll be true for a *lot* of revelations. You'll have to experience what you experience, Aur, and make your own sense of it. Now, go ahead and enjoy your meal. Fill up."

Leaning against the starboard gunwale she studies the water, the islands, the coastal landscape, the mountains capped in ice and snow, the endless verdure. Though we have another hour until sunset, Sol has eased behind the ridge line of Admiralty, dropping us into shadow. No one speaks another word until we reach a dock at the easternmost curve of Young Bay, and the Lords tie off the boat.

Another stone-laid path leads us through the trees, over a short peninsula, and into a massive clearing. I stop here, slack-jawed, goggling and unable to explain what's before me.

Thirteen meters above the high-tide line, a junkyard extends seven hundred meters toward the island's interior. It's a kilometer wide, a mountain of metals, plastics, and ceramics—

> drones,
> rockets,
> robots,
> automated vehicles,
> missile tubes,
> chassis,
> rotors,
> bombshells,

—and military scraps of every kind.

"What is this place?" I ask.

"I told you," says Bettina, "a graveyard."

"Looks more like a trash heap."

"What makes a grave?" Her smile taunts me. "The body inside it? Or the soul which has escaped it?"

"I'm an atheist." My breath lacks force, my lungs weak as paper bags.

She laughs. "Perfect. Then what's the difference between a meat machine and a metal machine?"

Most if not all these machines would have carried artificially intelligent systems, would have followed the guidance of remote pilots or would have flown under their own impetus. Is an AI a kind of soul? To someone who doesn't believe in souls, does it matter?

Some of these scraps bear the corporate markings of Avidità. Mr. Avidità has said as much, that over the Panhandle our machines tend to disappear.

"How do these end up here?" I ask.

"The Old Gods put them here," she says.

"Gods, huh? I'm surprised you're not salvaging the scrap."

"Sometimes the Horned Lords will scour for conventional explosives. We recover a lot of the titanium, too, have gotten pretty good at melting it down, reworking it." She gestures to one of the Lord's spearheads.

A sonic boom smacks over us. I flinch and a secondary *boom* rolls past, followed by pluming dust. A column of ejecta bursts from the graveyard's heart.

"Most of what's here was manufactured by Nesteler," Bettina explains. She wipes the dust from her eyes, then says, "They keep adjusting their technologies, increasing their speeds, but the Gods swallow their devices or break them apart before anything gets close."

My tumbling laugh surprises me. "This is insane," I say, "all of it."

"The Gods bring us everything but the nuclear warheads. Isn't that something?"

"Something?!" I run my hands through my hair, turn from her, try to find some perspective on what I'm experiencing. All this, well outside the precepts of biology, information theory, thermodynamics, chemistry, physics, basic epistemology. "Insane, all of it insane. Insane."

"You're right, Aur. Everything is insane. By definition. It's been insane a long, long, long time. Since before you were born."

I don't bother explaining what *born* means to me.

"Before *I* was born," she adds. "Before the birth of England, before the unification of China, before the building of the Great Pyramid. I've gotta tell you, Aur, it's been absolutely insane from the moment monkeys figured out how to light their own fires."

The sky deepens into mauve, a brushstroke of orange across the west, silhouetting Admiralty's peaks. An owl hoots.

"Prometheus," says Bettina, "was an asshole."

The Horned Lords chuckle.

"Ready to head back?" asks the Queen.

Rubbing my chin, I turn to her and nod. There must still be rational explanations.

"If she wants you," Bettina says, starting back down the path toward the docks and our waiting boat, "you can share Ruby's bed tonight. My guess is she's not done with you. My guess is she'd like to fuck you like an animal."

"I—" I don't know what to say.

"If she doesn't," adds Bettina, "just remember that *no* really does mean no."

I'm the last to leave the scrapyard. Its contours disappear in the deepening dark. I trail behind the Horned Lords, who don't seem in the slightest worried I might jump them from behind.

I think of Imka. I think of Ruby. I remember the epidemiological reports from San Francisco and Mr. Avidità's every word about sexually transmitted diseases.

XXIV. A SENDING

2131.4.14.7:12 PST
58°15'52.8"N 134°28'24.3"W
Alt 632m
The Faen
New Juneau
Hall of the Queens

I AWAKE IN RUBY's bed, and she is sitting, as conscious of her nakedness as a bird might be of its plumage. Outside the Hall of the Queens, angry male voices grunt, shout, growl, yell. The raven known as Evermore caws. All this noise rings throughout the square.

"What's going on?" I ask Ruby.

Her voice trembles. "A Sending."

"What is *that?*"

"Death to our enemies, that's what. You should see it."

I slide from her bed and dress. Two Horned Lords stand by the thrones, a few residents remain in their bowers, but everyone else has departed. The massive doors stand ajar, and I head out onto the steps.

A thousand citizens of New Juneau pack the outer edges of the square but leave open a wide area at its middle. The market which filled this space yesterday is gone. The Queens stand amidst sixteen Horned Lords, and I have arrived during Cailín's speech:

"—odens lend you His wisdom and guide you, you beloved brothers, lovers, teachers, guardians. Our loves. Our saviors—"

Bettina walks among the sixteen. They stand tall, grasping their spears, their focus soft.

"—and keepers. Our husbands. Your every wit, your every clever cut. Your best blades, you truest words, your conniving. Take every tool you have, every weapon, every trick, and bring the Gods—"

Bettina kisses the Horned Lords, kisses each as a bride would kiss her groom.

"—to Our enemies. This journey will be difficult, and the New Gods' magics are many and deceitful. Yet the Old Gods are with you, Our Gods of the millennia, who've seen everything before and will see everything again. They'll walk and battle and die beside you, Our brothers, and when all is done We'll join you in their Summer Country."

The Horned Lords rattle their spears and thump the cobbled ground with them. They grunt and howl. Purple froth spills from their mouths and dribbles through their beards. They convulse. One drops to his knees and vomits, the bile dark. They shout in the tongue I do not understand, the words packed with rage.

"Go," Cailín tells them, "honor the Gods, for Gods you are."

It's a biological weapon, I'm sure, whatever infects these people. Probably infects the land too, something altering the expression of proteins in plants *and* animals. The kind of shit Nesteler would do.

Maybe I can collect more samples, find a way to transport them to San Francisco, get them to the Bioengineering Division—

The Horned Lords growl and howl and crow. They shake as if trying to throw off their own skins. En masse the onlookers chant, though I cannot distinguish the mantra.

"Gods you are," says Cailín, lifting her hands toward the Horned Lords, "now fly!"

Quietly, tranquilly, softly the sixteen Lords explode. Not in fire but in feathers, blackbirds erupt where men had stood, their wings flapping madly into the sky. I try to count, but in the chaos their number defies me—hundreds—and no men remain. Not their bodies, their clothes, nor their spears appear to have survived this old-fashioned metamorphosis. Like the Goddesses Circe and Callisto, the Queens stand at the heart of the square, surrounded by a thousand witnesses.

Not a biological weapon. Not *only*, and whatever technology this is, well—

"Sufficiently advanced," I say.

Cailín waves to the crowds, then strolls back toward the hall. Passing me, she lays her hand on my shoulder.

"Keep looking for your rational explanations, spaceman."

She goes inside and the crowds disperse.

Before following her wife, Bettina winks at me. "Prepare for a journey, Aur. Enjoy a meal, relax, but we'll be sailing before one o'clock. We have a celebration to attend."

She leaves me alone in the afternoon sun. A few of the men-turned-blackbirds are still visible, high in the sky, heading south. Soon, however, the last disappears from view.

XXIV. ATTACHMENTS

Recollected

I MKA'S DEATH SHOOK ME. I often imagine that, if I'd been there, I could have saved her.

When we first got to know each other I was barely a teenager, and we enjoyed each other's company only another dozen times, mostly on Africa IV. She was thirty years my senior, though the first time I saw her I guessed the difference more like ten. Despite the chasm in our ages, I'd crafted my own fantasy about us falling in love, about us having children, about Mr. Avidità releasing me to live the life she and I wanted. To this day I'm not sure whether as a Harque I can have children or not, but with her I'd have happily tried.

After our third or fourth encounter, Imka would always greet me with "Hey, rabbit-keeper."

"Hey, lion-keeper," I'd reply.

I suspect she thought of me like an enthusiastic younger brother, but I took what I could get.

She died five years ago, on a run between the Asteroid Belt and High Earth Orbit. A Nesteler Warhawk destroyed her shuttle, the *Teetotaler*, though Imka probably never knew she was in danger, would have passed from *existence* to *nonexistence* in a millisecond.

On occasion I *still* find myself fantasizing.

What if?

What if we'd grown close in some other universe?

This is all *telling*, of course, and no *showing*. There's little substance in these recollections. Terrible for a Harque, who must live his narratives over and over until death, to assign such personally important events to exposition. But so it is. I wasn't there for Imka's death but, if I had been, I would've died with her.

There's not a damn thing I could've done to save anyone on the *Teetotaler*.

Flapjacks died earlier, of course, when I was eighteen. An old rabbit, almost twelve. I wasn't there for that moment either.

He faded peacefully in his hutch, surrounded by his food and his toys, one of the happiest rabbits to have ever lived.

My namesake once wrote, *Accept humbly, let go easily.*

Great advice, hellishly difficult in practice.

XXV. GIANTS & UNICORNS

2131.4.14.17:04 PST
57°13'29.2"N 133°45'46.7"W
Alt Sea Level
The Faen

THE QUEENS ASSEMBLED A company of dozens—men, women, children—and ordered the preparation of six boats. The flurry of tasks, the chaos and excitement they created, allowed no time for reflection, to either refute or accept the impossibilities I've seen.

"You," said an old sailor, his skin like loose canvas, his beard wild as sea foam, "you look like you're in need of usefulness."

"I guess I am," I replied.

I accompanied him to the docks. I'm not ignorant of sailing, but I know it in theory more than in practice. Not unkindly, the man barked his commands at me—

"Draw the pintles from the gudgeons!"

"Secure the tiller!"

"Organize the tack!"

—and I did as well as I could. Together we bent on the sail, tied the halyard to the jib, and ran the sheet. Yesterday I figured myself a dead man; the day before, an assassin; the day before that, a man who understood his place in the cosmos, one with a clear purpose and clearer loyalties.

Today is frictionless. I can't hold it, can't delineate my own identity. We know who we are, don't we? But when reality goes tits up, well—

I followed the sailor's directions until he declared the vessel seaworthy. It was a small single-sailed cutter, not more than a few years old but also from another time, crafted by hand from oakwood. Other teams prepared other boats, including a grander longship for the Queens and a high-tech yacht, a hydrofoil christened the *Potestatem,* the same which Bettina and Cailín once commandeered from San Francisco.

Now four hours later we're kilometers south, sailing under a steady wind. I ride at the starboard of the longship, near its impressive mast. Its sails billow, tugging us askew to the prevailing winds, and we bounce and chop against the waves. Bettina and Cailín perch nearer the prow. Nothing motorized on this vessel—men work the rigging and two stout women manage the rudder.

The hydrofoil plays outrider, clipping at our periphery, running circles around us. It had once belonged to the CEO of Strickland Industries, one of Avidità's subsidiaries. The boat carries quasi-military armaments, the kind capable of transforming coastlines into firestorms.

The Queens and their Horned Lords have had years to scavenge naval ports, to collect whatever the pre-Blight militaries had left behind.

Our route takes us through Stephens Passage, between the wooded hillsides of a dozen major islands. After Pulse Three and the drowning of the world's coasts, many a shoreline underwent radical alterations: the Inland Central Sea, east of San Francisco; the Eyre Australian Sea; Indonesia, and so many other low-lying geographies. Include in this accounting the Pacific Northwest and the Alaskan Panhandle, whose eroded valleys met the rising waters, erasing a hundred islands while creating a thousand more. These new isles dot the waters through which we glide, but I doubt most have a name. Mysterious, each one, imbued with romances, as if on them I might meet Oberon and Titania.

The lithe, skinnier, agile cutters ride lower in the water. They'd be fearsome weapons of war—in the ninth century—and the majority of their passengers aren't warriors anyway. Artisans or farmers, not killers.

They don't carry many personal weapons either.

Axes. Spears. A few hunting rifles.

I've been wondering where the machine guns are? The rocket launchers? The killbots?

Why is it that Avidità or Nesteler or the UPRC hasn't wiped the Faen from existence? One tactical nuke would do it.

The Gods bring us everything but the nuclear warheads, Bettina had said. I *saw* the graveyard of technology.

On the nearest cutter sits Alastar's new nurse, and she tucks the baby against her breast. Another child is with her, a brown-skinned, wiry-haired toddler. Near her is a third child, a pale sticklike girl of about seven, her dark hair long and straight. Of all things, she cradles a fluffy white puppy to her chest, and a darker pup plays at her feet.

We navigate from the Passage into Frederick Sound. Fog rolls in from the Pacific, wreathing the Baranof Islands, Kuiu Islands, and Kupreanof Islands in cream-white clouds, muting shades of evergreen into one hue undercut by inexplicable violets.

For seven glorious minutes the dusk transforms the sky, clouds shot through by kaleidoscopic rays like the trumpets of Valkyries riding home to Sessrúmnir.

Yet in the moments after dusk deepens into twilight, these metaphors lose meaning. No romances. No Oberon or Titania. No Norse Goddesses astride winged horses.

These fantasies shed their power, crushed by a giant who lumbers at the darkening horizon.

A giant.

THIS IS NOT A METAPHOR.

I stand and the ship's rocking threatens to toss me overboard. Clutching my chest, I squint, convincing myself that what I see *is* what I see.

Both there and *not* there, the giant towers with its globulous head amongst the cloud-faded moonlight. Its colossal mass defies reason, a tentacled under-the-bed nightmare grown to Godhood. Winglike forms stretch from its back, translucent, tricking my eye—I cannot say where they end and the sky begins.

A WADING GIANT.

It sloshes northward through the ocean the way a man might shuffle through a kiddie pool. The islands and clouds and coming nighttime obscure my view, but I guess the giant must be following the continental shelf, past the drowned city of Sitka, one hundred klicks away.

"Sit," says Cailín, sliding onto the bench beside me.

"What the fuck *is* that?" I ask, unable to look away from the mountainous, fleshy shoggoth.

"Sit."

I button my fleece and join her. As Sol disappears, its warmth does too. Along much of the equator, April will see many days hotter than forty-five Celsius, but at this latitude that's hard to imagine. Cailín's cloak wraps her and in it she resembles some as-yet-uncategorized arctic mammal.

Waves smack the hull, a lulling rhythm, and I glance back over my shoulder to find the giant shoggoth gone. Veiled by fog? Submerged? A figment of my imagination?

"You're questioning your sanity," says Cailín.

I am but I say, "No—"

"To survive you'll need a touch of madness."

"Giants do not wander the oceans," I say. "Men don't turn into birds. Monsters don't eat sacrificial victims."

Her look is incredulous. "Monsters have *always* eaten sacrificial victims."

"The Minotaur or Cetus or Scylla, they're not real—"

"Any large corporation, any war, any drug epidemic—"

"Not the same."

"Isn't it?"

She sets her hand on my thigh, so overfamiliar I startle. I'd retreat, if I could, but nothing except the gunwale intervenes between me and the Sound's near-freezing waters. Could I make it to shore before succumbing to the cold?

"What is a unicorn?" Cailín asks me.

"This a trick question? A horse or goat with a single horn, growing from its forehead."

She rolls her eyes. "Assume they don't exist."

"Do they?" Would it be such a surprise?

"Assume they don't. What *is* a unicorn?"

"An allegory," I say.

"Excellent!" Her Irish inflections sparkle with delight. "For what?"

I shrug. "Purity, innocence, enchantment. Unicorns only visit virgins," I say, "so the moral is to remain pure if you want magic in your life."

"Lovely child's fable, isn't it? What is a corporation?"

I narrow my eyes at her. "Corporations *do* exist."

Sitting back in mock surprise, she blinks at me. "Could we hunt one tomorrow, shoot it through the heart, roast it, slice it up, serve it on a plate, and *eat* it?"

"Uh—"

"I've never *eaten* a corporation before! Marvelous! I can't wait to taste one."

"You're razzing me."

"Such an *American* word, 'razzing.' Listen, a unicorn could be *more* real than a corporation. Everyone on this ship could say, 'I don't believe in unicorns,' but if a unicorn met us ashore, we'd have to change our minds, wouldn't we?"

"I suppose."

"What of corporations? If everyone who believes in them decided there was no such thing—" She snaps her fingers.

"Not sure that follows."

Even the UPRC uses corporations, owned in majority by the state, and corporations outlive their founders—Avidità excepted. As near as I can tell, corporations are *more* real than some humans.

Cailín tucks a wisp of her hair behind her ear, but the wind insists on freeing it. "Monsters exist," she says.

"Your wife said something about you making *pacts* with them. How do you enforce such agreements? How do you make a deal with Charybdis?"

"By serving something just as powerful."

"Nodens," I say.

"The Elder Gods!" She claps her hands, delighted. "You're a spy, spaceman, in a world which won't suffer lies, and you haven't the faintest idea what you're doing."

I have an ego, but I brush aside her words. "When did you know what I was?"

"We had you *made*—that *is* the correct word, 'made,' isn't it?—shortly after you crossed into the Faen."

"How?"

She touches her thumb to my forehead in the same way the Horned Lord did, that night at Threshold. No pain this time, her touch almost sensual.

"In the Faen," she says, "lies are difficult to tell."

"Does that mean you see the truth?"

"We know what Nodens wishes us to know, and there is *no* fooling Him."

I lean against the gunwale, considering the leap over it, into the water. Portside behind Cailín sits a Horned Lord, not looking my way, but making his presence felt. I'm as much a prisoner as I would be with shackles around my wrists.

"What do you know about me?" I ask her.

"You arrived in an Avidità-made escape pod—"

I correct her. "A re-entry lozenge."

"You're a terrible assassin but a good errand boy. The infant, Alastar, came down with you, though we found the farm and all the corpses, as you described them. Staged?"

It's too dark to discern details across the water. Whether Alastar and his new caretaker still sit in the open or have gone beneath their vessel's canvas covers, I don't know.

"I'm confused," I say.

"Why?" says Cailín, laying her hand on mine.

I'm beginning to understand, though. Cailín is a mother to this community, she *embodies* it, while her wife embodies some darker instinct for sheer survival. Yet Cailín, too, exudes a darkness, deep and as lightless as the Taku Inlet, as the sea floor, as the Mariana Trench. I'm reminded—*Water seeks the dark places, where no one wishes to go. In the deep places it is closest to the true way.*

Not my namesake's words, but I've always found a complementary tension between the *Tao Te Ching* and the *Meditations of Marcus Aurelius.*

"Why am I still alive?" I ask.

"The Old One rejected you—"

"I'm a spy," I say. "You *knew* I was."

"What would Thomas Avidità do with an enemy spy?"

"A spy wouldn't suffer, much. Mr. Avidità has ways of interrogating that don't cause much pain."

She laughs. "Avidità, the lesser of evils."

The Lesser of Evils.

A new Avidità corporate tagline?

"Compared to the UPRC? Nesteler?" I say. "Sure. But the two of you, you're as evil."

"How do you reckon?"

"Summary justice, the violent raids, the shit your Horned Lords do, reaching as far down as California now—"

"No such thing as California. Today there's only the Fáen and everything which isn't yet the Fáen."

"You make my point for me," I say. "You sound like Caesar or Genghis Khan or Hitler."

Cailín eyes me. "Don't ever make *those* comparisons again."

"All right," I say.

"If you survive here long enough, you'll come to understand."

"How do I do that?"

"Come to understand?"

"Survive."

Cailín's hand, still resting in mine, squeezes reassuringly. "What was your mission here?"

Is it treason, saying it? "First, to deliver the baby to you."

"Why?"

"Truthfully, I don't know."

"What else?" she asks.

"To go to Wrangell Island, to discover what's there."

She laughs. "Lucky you! We're on our way there now."

"Is that coincidence? Dumb luck?"

"What do you think?" After a moment she asks, "Anything else you were supposed to accomplish, besides putting a bullet through my head? Through my wife's head?"

"That wasn't Mr. Avidità's command, by the way."

"What *was* his command?"

"He left your deaths up to my discretion."

"You could've killed Bett, certainly. Why didn't you?"

"Too many unanswered questions, I suppose, questions about you, about what's happening down here. It's why Mr. Avidità let you and Bettina leave San Francisco. You make him curious."

"Do we make *you* curious?"

I nod.

She glances toward Bettina, her wife almost invisible in the failing light. "I'm grateful for your curiosity, Aur, and I'll do everything I can to satisfy it. You'll be the most knowledgeable ex-spy in all history."

Ex-spy.

"Anything else which Thomas Avidità commanded of you?" she asks.

"To return to him, alive, and give him a full report, to share with him everything I learn here."

She frowns, leans forward, and kisses my cheek. "There's little you're not going to learn, Aur, but I can tell you this— you'll never share a detail of it with your King."

At those words I pull away.

"Aur!" shouts Cailín. "No!"

In the dusk, with abominations in the sea and giants in the sky, with numbing temperatures and a changed landscape, with enemies all around me, I leap into the breath-stealing water. It closes over my head and ices my veins.

Yet I swim for the nearest moonlit shore.

XXVI. VISIONS, PART VI

LONG AFTER SUNRISE I find myself in a forest of spruce, ponderosa, cedar, and hemlock. Ferns and junipers blanket the forest floor, a palette of green above and green below, greens in a hundred tints and shades, greens shot through by the subtlest washes of violet. Throughout the understory, birds sing, more than I've ever before heard, even in Mr. Avidità's gardens, even in the terraria. Daylight glitters through the leaves, delectably bright, warming me to my core.

A spicy-sweet aroma drifts on a caressing breeze. Mint, sage, and *life* flavor everything.

Utterly alone, I wander this forest until a deer herd crosses my path. They leap a crystalline cascade, a stream spilling into an emerald meadow. Along the stream's banks grow raspberries, and I eat my fill.

A frightened rabbit bolts from the raspberry bushes, vanishing through the undergrowth, and I follow it.

At the meadow's far side, the forest constricts and in it, amidst a thicket of hawthorn, grows a twisted oak. From this oak a bleached skull hangs from a hemp rope, the knot tied through the eye sockets, the ethmoid bone between them pierced. Ravens circle the tree's crown.

I lift the skull and examine it. Jawless, it nonetheless grins at me.

Eight more skulls hang from this tree.

More oak trees grow behind it, a forest in a forest which seems impossibly old. From each tree hang nine more skulls, some fresh and white, others aged and mossy. In one tree the skulls still cling to spines. A rising breeze gently swings these floating ornaments, these airy dancers.

Ravens chatter. Speckles of summery light invade from above, but the shadows deepen and the woodland grows cooler. Ahead, past a hundred more oaks and nine hundred more skulls, another clearing awaits, announced in golden light.

Not knowing why, I hold my breath, choosing my steps carefully.

In the golden clearing stand stones of crisply worked white granite, each as tall as a man, arranged in a circle around a fire pit. Charcoal and half-burnt logs fill the pit, while a fresher woodpile is nearby. At the circle's other side is the tallest oak I've ever seen, a hundred meters high at least, its boughs broad enough to shelter a soccer stadium. Two squirrels play tag in its bows and far above them perches an eagle.

The rabbit stands on a fat root, looks at me, then hops out of sight.

Seven corpses hang from this giant oak, stripped and bloodied, one without a right hand. Ribbons of blue, red, and purple flutter from the boughs. Sticks swing from the ribbons, tied into patterns I know I'll remember but whose meanings I do not know.

A fire burns in the pit. Was it burning before?

A woman sits by the fire. Was she there before?

She cooks pancakes on a cast-iron pan. There's batter and butter and maple syrup. On one rock warms a plate piled with flapjacks. On another hot stone steams an antiquated steel coffee pot.

I *know* these were not there before.

"Come sit with me, Aurelius."

Finding a spot opposite her, I say, "Where am I?"

"You're home."

I shake my head. "Home is Station."

She pours coffee into a mug and hands it to me. The coffee tastes strong, bitter, and sublime.

"Don't be ridiculous," she says. "The Stations are nothing but glorified mobile homes."

She serves up three pancakes, hands me a plate, and gives me a fork. Thick and buttery, the maple syrup runs down my throat.

After refilling my coffee, the woman sips her own. Her long, curly hair hangs madly across her shoulders. Her wide hips and ample bosom fill a royal-purple dress.

Ewe's horns curl from the sides of her head, spiraling around her ears. They're majestic, patterned in white and black. Were those there before?

"Who are you?" I ask.

"Your mother," she replies.

"I don't have a mother."

"You do now."

I shove another forkful of syrup-laden pancake into my mouth, wash it down with a gulp of coffee. "Mr. Avidità told me he couldn't give me a mother."

"Because you were dropped from some rubbery, stand-in vagina? Nonsense." She scrapes another pancake from the pan and adds it to the stack. "How're the flapjacks?"

"Delicious."

"Come closer, love, and let me take a better look at you."

I move around the fire, sit beside her, and set my plate and coffee aside. She rests her hands on my shoulders, her touch rich and reassuring. She licks her lips, lips the color of her dress. Her eyes, a darker and depthless violet, take me in.

Planting a kiss on my forehead, she says, "You're still young, Aurelius, and you've never *really* grown up. I know what you need."

My mouth feels dry, won't quite work, but I manage to form the words: "What do I need?"

"Tell me, Aurelius, what would make you happiest? What have you ever wished for—besides your mother—that you could never have?"

The image of my desire comes instantly to mind. An African savanna far distant from Africa, of everything and everyone I encountered there.

To my left, Imka sits down.

Was she there before?

"Hey, rabbit-keeper," she says.

"Hey, lion-keeper."

We eat together, plenty of breakfast to be had. Imka talks incessantly and dazzlingly of her terrarium, and of the lions most of all. I love her every word.

"They ask about you sometimes," she says.

"The lions?" I ask.

"Yes."

Mother clears the plates and food. Inside the circle she stretches blankets.

Imka is beautiful, her hair dark and saintly, her earthy eyes bright and lively, her curves fitted perfectly to the contours of my memory. She kisses me and I return her kiss. We kiss again and our kisses lead one into another, kisses inviting our hands, inviting our tongues. We toss aside our clothes and mother adds them to the fire.

In a torrent of caresses I find myself under Imka and I fill her. She rides me, her dance selfish, taking her pleasure in every wave of her hips, yet her selfishness gives back to me a thousandfold.

Mother walks the circle. She talks to the birds and to the trees. Are her hooves cloven?

"Come, come," she says, laughing, "find happiness, my children."

We do.

I spill myself inside Imka, and she exacts one last small death for herself. Mother is a Goddess and she fills the circle, fills the clearing, fills the wood. Pure shadow, she fills the spaces between the light.

Darkness is *not* the absence of light.

She fills the spaces inside us.

"Do not be concerned," she says to us. "Your suffering is temporary, children, but the Summer Country is forever."

From her dress she draws thread and a curved needle. The needle is like a whaling hook; the thread, like a hangman's rope. She forces these through my eyes, behind the bridge of my nose, skewering flesh and bone. The crunching echoes between my ears, and I am screaming, shrieking, lifted up where I swing, back and forth, side to side, my head ratcheted, the pain an absolute white flame. One more death upon the tree and, though blind, I know Imka hangs beside me.

"Shh, children," says mother. "I'm with you. I am Nodens, and I'll never abandon you."

There are sublime magics in this pain. If I can concentrate hard enough, maybe I can remember them, but the *pain*—

—my screams continue.

Besides, I don't believe in magic, do I?

"Why all the caterwauling?" Nodens says. "No need for it. You know this is only a dream—"

2131.4.15.6:24 PST
56°27'05.6"N 132°22'17.4"W
Alt 3m
The Faen
Inside Passage

I WAKE SCREAMING AND painfully cold.

Hours ago, after swimming to land, I sheltered in the overgrown branches beneath several old pines. To stave off the hypothermia, I stripped off my soaked clothes and I've wrapped myself in the fleece coat which, most critically, sheds water. Before passing out I'd managed to cover myself in rotting foliage, glad for its insulation.

Now, awake again, I can at least draw a full breath. Though numbed, my fingers and toes and testicles and penis continue to report their existence, and I don't believe I'll be losing anything to frostbite. My muscles are no longer seizing.

Still I'm shivering, my teeth clicking. Also that goddamned dream remains with me.

Pancakes?

Flapjacks.

It's not yet sunrise but the clouds have dissipated and the stars shine, allowing me to recalibrate the local time and my location. An aurora borealis glimmers across the northern horizon, obfuscated by trees, but it soon fades and leaves only weak moonlight behind it, low on the western horizon. I find myself waiting for sunrise, and I hope the clear skies mean a comfortable morning. Maybe I'll be able to dry my clothes, clear my head, and formulate a plan.

From the south, mournful howls roll across the landscape.

I've heard wolves before. That wasn't wolves. Something bigger.

Now's the time to formulate my plan.

How to reach San Francisco?

Make my way inland, the long way through Prince George?

Or by sea?

Calculating distances, speed of travel, survival odds—ordinarily simple equations, now challenging. My teeth clatter more, the temperature holding a few degrees above freezing.

A fire would help, but it carries its own risks, doesn't it? Light to be seen, drifting smoke.

I'm *so* cold.

Below an old ponderosa I scrounge for duff, manage to gather twigs dry enough to snap. It's difficult to concentrate on anything other than the task at hand. I split a larger stick, tap the duff into it, dig a shallow hole into the loam, and rub a narrower length of wood against it. Friction is key, and to protect my fingers I wrap them in a length of my tunic. After twenty minutes, even through the fabric, the wood grows hot. My thumb will blister, but I keep working, catching a whiff of smoke.

A second time, howls coil through the forest. Closer.

Must work faster.

The smoke curls past my face, a flame sparks, and I shelter it with my hands, adding more duff. The spark grows to a palm-sized fire. To this I add several twigs; to the twigs, sticks; to the sticks, small branches. The flames crackle. Gently, carefully, reverently I lay a small log beside the flames, not on them, and lean two more across the first. The logs are moist and there'd been no way for me to split them. If I burn through my tinder before the larger pieces light, the fire will die.

I keep adding twigs. Water vapor joins the smoke, and the bark hisses and sweats and pops. More twigs. At last, flames lick one log, then another, and I nurse these until they blacken. With more confidence, I add a bigger log, too long for the pit I've dug, but one which I can feed into the flames.

Across the range, howls answer each other, one due south, the other southeast. *Much* closer.

The fire roars, its radiance luscious, while pins and needles prickle my warming extremities. I drape my soaked clothes and fleece coat across nearby branches, setting them near enough the flames to dry.

Dawn arrives in this Land of the Gods. The eastern trees gain definition, pines mostly, but a dozen deciduous species capture the early light. The Morning Star—the Goddess Venus—outshines everything else in the sky and I can almost imagine Aphrodite descending into this forest.

By my estimates, I'm on the northwest extension of Wrangell. East of here, the Inside Passage fractures into narrower channels, though I'd rather *not* swim island to island to the mainland. This means I'll need a raft, something flat with a ballast and a basic oar.

Hell, something I could build in a day.

I *am* near the source of Bettina's and Cailín's old tracking devices, the very point which Mr. Avidità wanted me to investigate, but the Queens and their entourage are also on this island, somewhere, maybe with others. I know enough already to make my report, and all I want is to leave.

Howls again. Hard to pinpoint the direction.

These sound like some fucking *large* animals, and I feed more wood into the fire. It roars now, a strong blaze, pushing back the understory's shadows while the sunlight brightens the treetops.

I stretch and turn to drive away the cold.

I'm a spaceman come to Earth, stripped of unearthly contraptions, squatting in the most primeval forest I can imagine. A few days' stubble roughens my face.

Howls.

I should have come with stealthware, with fiber armor, with full-spectrum sensory augmentation, with explosives, with laz-guns, with personal drones, with AIs. Then again I shouldn't have come at all. Any of my brothers would be better prepared for this.

Hell, right now I'd kill for a knife.

Instead I choose the strongest, straightest, sharpest fallen branch I can find. As the east burnishes into gold, I refine the spearpoint by grinding it against stone, then hold it into the fire to char and harden. It's a poor spear, even by prehistoric standards, but I'm confident I could ram it through a flank of meat.

A blazing fire and a spear. I feel properly savage.

Fifteen meters from me, standing on a lichen-covered boulder as if she'd been there all night, a familiar girl watches me. Her purple dress covers her from her throat to her ankles and wrists. Leather boots protect her feet. Nothing industrially manufactured, the boots nonetheless appear expertly crafted. A fur cloak wraps her shoulders and drapes her to her thighs. Her height and frame suggest she's seven, maybe eight. Her expression strikes me as serious. Her dark hair fans across the mantle of her cloak.

"Hi," I say, "I noticed you on the boat."

She can't be alone. Adults must be nearby, but I hear no one.

"You're the one named Aurelius," she says.

"Yeah."

Her eyes! *Absurdly* blue, the exact shade of her mother's.

"Why'd you jump ship?" she asks.

"I need to go home."

"You *are* home. Don't you know?"

"What's *your* name?"

"Eagna."

"Nice name." I gesture to my clothes, still sopping, and to myself, a grown man embarrassed by a girl. "I'm sorry, I'm not prepared for a royal visit, princess."

She hops off the boulder and steps toward me. "My mothers aren't here."

Eagna doesn't seem to mind that I look like a half-drowned mole rat. Neither does she care about the spear I carry.

"Where are they?" I ask.

"Half an hour walk," she says, "preparing the rites to Eostre."

It *is* Easter today.

"I admit, I hadn't expected that."

Finally, she smiles. "Won't you come with me, Aurelius? Everyone's worried about you. You *must* celebrate with us," she says, not as a command but as if I might be crushingly disappointed if I don't take her advice.

"I've got friends waiting for me. I must go."

Eagna shakes her head. "What are you?"

"What do you mean?" I add more wood to the fire, encourage it back to a roar.

"What *are* you? You're not human, well, not a *normal* human."

"How do you know?"

"I smell it," she says. "You're *mostly* human, but you're bits of other things too."

"DNA splices," I explain. "Some from other organisms, some engineered from scratch. You know what DNA is?"

"Not really." She scrunches her lips and her eyes narrow.

"I'm what's called a *Harque.*"

"What's a hark?"

"Spelled with a Q-U-E. A Harque is a kind of record keeper, an observer, an advisor."

Her head tilts.

I continue, "Avidità Corporation relies on computers, but computers can be hacked and falsified. Neither blockchaining nor quantum computing have stopped viruses or malware. Some Harques provide a biological checksum, ensure the AI are reporting correctly, doing what their owners directed them to do."

Her brow furrows.

"I'm sorry," I say. "I'm sure none of that made sense."

"You don't forget things."

"Not much. It's called an *eidetic* memory."

"You'll remember everything we're saying now?"

I nod. "I keep a running narrative, going on in my head, all the time."

Imagine she's tasted a sour lemon—that's her expression. I *almost* laugh.

"I don't think *you're* much of a normal human either," I say.

She tilts her head the other way.

"An educated guess," I say.

"The Horned Lord says your memory is interesting."

"Does he?"

"But He says your heart is much *more* interesting."

"Why?"

"Because you're good."

I frown. "I'm not sure about that."

"Why?"

"I've killed a lot of people."

"You don't enjoy it."

"No."

Eagna nods. *"Please* come with me now. No need to kill anyone. There'll be breakfast waiting."

"Tempting," I say, "but I can't. My friends *are* expecting me."

"You mean Thomas Avidità?"

My breath catches—she must have talked with her mother? "Yes."

"You'll tell him everything you've seen and heard, everything you've learned, and what you tell him will be true and correct."

Has my heart dropped into my intestines? "You're a smart and articulate girl, you know that, Eagna?"

"I cannot let you go to Thomas Avidità." She steps closer.

"You're smart," I say, "but you're also small, and there's not much you can do to stop me. Head back to your mothers. By the time you reach them, by the time they can send anyone to retrieve me, I'll be long gone."

So much for fashioning a raft. No time. I'll have to swim for it.

"My mothers aren't here," she says, "but I'm not alone."

Shit.

I grasp the spear.

"I brought my puppies," she says.

The two fluff-balls, the little dogs beside her during the voyage from New Juneau. Laughing, I let go my breath.

"Take your puppies back with you," I say. "Now, go! My clothes have got a bit more drying to do."

Raising her face to the brightening morning sky, Eagna howls. Two more howls join her little-girl voice, songs like war horns, elemental and *near*. The first pale wolflike beast leaps onto the boulder behind her. The second, its fur a mottled charcoal gray, emerges from the trees to the north.

Lithe animals with long snouts. Shaggy. Toothy but neither dogs nor wolves.

Tall as horses.

Eagna holds out her small hand toward me. "Come with us, Aurelius."

I stand, clutching my shoddy spear with both hands, and I position the fire between me and the beasts. They hesitate to approach, come no closer, as frightened by fire as any other animal.

The little girl gestures toward the flames, as if brushing dust from the air, and they go out. Snuffed. Only tendrils of smoke.

I run. I run my ass off. I run faster than I've ever run before.

Recollected
2131.3.21.20:12 GMT
Alt 40.1E6m
High Earth Orbit
EIK-Cel Station

MR. Avidità hunkered over a bioengineering workstation. He dissected an organism I didn't recognize, nothing I'd ever studied in any textbook. Fleshy, eight legs, a tail, no discernible head, probably endoskeletal. Its underbelly looked vulval.

"Thank you for coming," he said to me, not looking up from his microscope.

I never responded to such questions. If the King summoned me, I went. His thank yous amounted to ceremony.

The room's speaker system was playing the last bars of Radiohead's 2016 "Burn the Witch".

AIs ran the biolabs, monitored the million-million daily splices, the unending recombinations of raw genetic material. Only one in ten billion resulted in a viable organism, but that meant the labs invented a hundred new creatures per day.

"This is an interesting one," said Mr. Avidità, folding back a wet flap of skin-like material, revealing a fleshy tube.

"Looks like a wasp's ovipositor," I said, "a few orders of magnitude larger."

"Superficially."

"What can I do for you, Your Grace?"

So much white! Every surface in the biolabs shone as whitely as possible. White for pure. White for clean. White for sterile. White reassured the lab's few technicians. If blood or some other bodily fluid escape its confines, splattered where it wasn't supposed to go, *white* revealed it.

I stood at ease, hands crossed behind my back, waiting for Mr. Avidità to answer me. The music shifted into Cabal Monkey's 2073 masterpiece, "Racial Facial". White. The irony.

"We've accumulated more than enough genetic material on the Stations," he said, "to ensure the survival of humanity for a thousand generations. In the terraria, we have two-thirds of all species known to exist at the beginning of the twenty-first century—not exactly a Noah's Ark, but frankly our Arks aren't mythological bullshit."

"Yes, Your Grace."

Why'd he summon me? I didn't have many hours before I, and the baby, would launch from Station and drop into Earth's atmosphere. Mr. Avidità continued his dissection, snipping one leg from the odd creature on his bench, setting the limb aside.

"We estimate," he said, "all species which have ever existed represent less than one-one-trillionth of one percent of all DNA-based life which could ever evolve. Isn't that remarkable?"

No joke. That so many organisms might, statistically speaking, emerge from DNA's matrix—nothing short of mind-blowing.

"It is, Your Grace."

"You might be wondering," he said, "the real purpose of your mission?"

"You've always discouraged me from asking about such things."

He chuckled. "Crèche-born aren't supposed to know a goddamned thing about the purposes of their missions. You're to know the *what,* the *how,* the *when,* and the *where,* but never the *why.* All the black-op bullshit your brothers are doing these days, you think they've got the faintest clue why they're slaughtering the residents of the Xīwàng Orbiter? Or crushing Nesteler on Ceres? No, they do not."

He incised the creature's tail, examining its tendons, identifying unusual interlinkages between its vertebrae.

"You're different, Aur. You've always been different. You're sensitive, discerning. You appreciate subtleties. You'd choose a rabbit over an empire."

"Doesn't that make me foolish, Your Grace?"

He laughed, looked up from his microscope, and set down his tools. "It makes you the smartest goddamned motherfucker of the lot of us."

I waited.

He continued, "If whatever's going on in the Alaskan Panhandle is the work of the UPRC or, more so, if it's some Nesteler project—fuck 'em. I *need* to know what's going on down there, Aur. Diplomatic attempts with the Queens have failed. Our drones don't last more than five minutes inside their *airspace,* which as near as I can tell has no planes, no drones, and no conventional ground-to-air defenses. I mean, what the fuck? They capture my spies quickly enough too. Hell, you might be no exception there."

This startled me. "You don't have faith in me, Your Grace?"

"You're the apple of my eye, Aur, but so far those bitches have sniffed out every single goddamned thing I've thrown at them. Still, I've got an intuition with you."

"An *intuition?*"

He shrugged and turned back to his work. "You're the man for the job, right?"

"You're risking my life on an intuition?"

"Yes, Aur, I am."

Ever had to swallow a pill that wouldn't quite go down? That you had to force, that hurt all the way to your stomach?

"You going to tell me the *why?*" I asked.

"If it's Nesteler," he said, "if it's the UPRC—"

"Fuck 'em. Yes, I got that part, Your Grace."

"But what if it's not?"

What if? I had nothing to say on the matter, hadn't thought of it, couldn't have said in that moment what it might mean if the phenomena—the change in surface condition, the Horned Lords, the Queens—weren't some other corporation's top-secret program.

The music transitioned into King Makis's 2019 "Re-Entry", a track bizarrely playful and grand and moody.

"What if it's not?" Mr. Avidità repeated. "Then we've got a real conundrum."

"Why?"

"It's almost always a mistake to destroy the unknown, to deny it your full attention. If whatever's going on down there has *nothing* to do with Nesteler or the UPRC, it might represent a new threat, but it might also offer us some new opportunity."

I nodded, as if I had the faintest idea what he meant.

He continued, "As I mentioned, Aur, we've got enough material to ensure the survival of humanity, but what the Earth needs is a fallow period."

"Your Grace?"

"What I mean is this—you know we invented Blight? Of course we didn't name it *Blight*. It's not like I brought the branding team together to dream up the best possible trademark for the end of civilization."

Was Station rocking? Was our orbit stable? Were we about to career into Earth's atmosphere?

Only my head spinning. I forced myself to take a long, slow, quiet breath.

"We *have* to save humanity," he said, "like we've got to save lions and elephants. But here's the trick—we also need to hit Earth's reset button."

I swallowed hard. "How do we accomplish that?"

"An ice age."

"What?"

"We're quite sure of the engineering."

"I'm actually not sure I understand, Your Grace."

"*An ice age.* I mean to cool the Earth to something like the late Pleistocene."

"That'll kill most of whoever's left down there."

"I've already killed a few billion," he said. "What's a few more million?"

My mouth was hanging open. I closed it—before it filled with flies.

"Here's the thing, Aur—" He made another incision, examined what appeared to be *two* livers. "If you infiltrate the Queen's territory, talk with Bett and Cailín, determine that what's happening down there is something *new*, I'll cancel or postpone the ice age, see if we can work something out with the Queens of the Horned Lord. If you assassinate them, or you report that the phenomena are the expression of a competitor's technologies, well—"

"Yes, Your Grace."

"Now you understand the *why?*"

I did.

"It's up to you, Aur. *Your* call, should you find yourself before the Queens." He split the creature's ribcage, examined its chest cavity. "If you decide there's something there which Avidità Corporation needs to understand better, well, you come back here and let me know."

"Otherwise?" I asked.

"I'm going to drop Earth's average temperatures by fourteen Celsius." Once more he looked up at me. "You're my man. Don't think of the weight as being on your shoulders, though. The decision to strike the final blow, to obliterate what's left of humanity on Earth, that'll be mine. The only power I'm giving you," he said, "is to stay the execution."

Sodom and Gomorrah, I thought.

"Go on," said Mr. Avidità, tugging an eight-chambered heart from the organism's chest, "make your final preparations."

"Yes, Your Grace."

For one more moment the dissected creature held my attention, then I departed for the crèche.

XXIX. EASTER HUNT

2131.4.15.7:48 PST
56°27'05.6"N 132°22'17.4"W
Alt 7m
Wrangell Island
The Faen

EAGNA'S PUPPIES DON'T YET give chase but I am *flying,* full sprint, into the thickest growths of pine I can find. I choose any land over which horse-sized predators might not be able to stretch their legs, but I'm not sure how much ground I can cover either.

You try running naked and barefoot through wet forests scarcely above freezing, see how *you* do. The adrenaline does all the work, pushes the grisly reality to the back of my mind.

Don't think about what the rocks are doing to my feet.

Don't think about the branches and nettles against my bare skin.

Don't think about the maximum velocity of *any* canine.

At least I've dried off. Hell, I'm working up a sweat. Gripping my spear, I swing it like a dull machete, sweeping the greenery ahead, clearing the way. I enter a rock-strewn hollow, a series of pine-needle-blanketed bowls and sharp hillocks. My toes are bleeding.

Howls echo through the forests, the pitch raising the hairs on the back of my neck. Now they're coming.

I leap across boulders deposited an ice age ago, slick with moss and lichen. As I vault downed pines, tree trunks scattered across the craggy terrain like pickup sticks, a splintered branch catches me under the rubs and cuts deep.

Stumbling, skinning my knees, I keep moving. The howls close on me—fuck they're quick!—and I look for a new route, anywhere I might go that they can't. The boulders pile one atop another and I climb, climb, climb—

Stones arise from either side of a slender crevasse, a mere gash in the earth. Ferns and currants crowd the gap between the crevasse's edges of loose earth and granite. The bottom is three meters down.

I leap.

In the fall, the ferns slap my legs, my groin, my stomach. I roll and manage to regain my feet, spear still in hand. With my back wedged against stone, I guard the slender opening above. Impossible to flank me, to take me from any other direction, so I wait.

On either side of the crevasse, along its lip, the beasts appear. First the pale one—I'll think of him as Whitey—then the dark one, Blackie.

Past them, past the surrounding trees, the sky has brightened into a clean blue, promising a pleasant springtime afternoon.

Whitey lowers his furry head, growls, and lifts his hackles.

I brace the spear.

He springs for me and his jaws catch my left shoulder, but the spear slides into his chest, drives through lungs and heart, and bursts from his back. Two hundred fifty kilos of dead puppy pin me, and I slide to my ass. Whitey's blood bathes me.

Blackie circles the crevasse's lip. He growls, paces, seeks an angle of attack. In better circumstances—less injured, less exhausted, less trapped—I could lift Whitey's cadaver and return to my defensive position. Not so easy now.

After several failed attempts to dislodge the spear, I let it go. I manage to shove Whitey aside, but I have to twist myself, to turn my back to Blackie.

He growls, lowers his head into a space made tighter by his brother's corpse, and snaps at me. His drool slicks my shoulder.

I punch his nose. "Fuck you!"

After freeing my legs I crouch, sandwiched between the carcass on one side and the ravine wall on the other. Blackie snaps again, nearer my head.

My spear's point juts from Whitey's back. I could yank it free, maybe fight my way out—

—only speed will do—

—and I spring onto Whitey, wrap both hands around the spear's bloodied haft, plant my feet in Whitey's fur, and *pull.*

I pull with every gram of strength I've got, but I was never as strong as my brothers. The haft slides another meter from the body, but it snags a rib or catches the tough heart meat. I tug again, twist the spear between myself and Blackie—

He lunges.

His teeth catch my hip, yank me up, then lose their hold. Pain spreads white-hot across my flank and I fall, face down against Whitey's fur.

Blackie bites my left leg and this time his teeth puncture skin and muscle. I scream my lungs out. While I clamber at the crevasse's edge, the beast drags me. We teeter and I wrap my hands around the spear, not sure if I'm hoping for it to slip free or hold fast.

His teeth hit bone.

"Fuck!"

I lose my grip and rise above the crevasse. My fists fall on dark fur and hard muscle, and the beast carries me overland, dragging me by my leg. My blood flows hot, wet, and dark. Hauled over rocks, logs, roots, I keep screaming.

Of all the ways to die, I never imagined being eaten alive. My head strikes a slab of limestone—

Sedimentary. Calcium carbonate.

—and—

XXX. GROVE OF THE HORNED LORD

Unknown Time (Late Day, Assume Easter Day)
Unknown Location
Alt Unknown
Assume Wrangell Island
Assume the Faen

I F I HADN'T GOTTEN a concussion in the Hall of the Queens, I'm pretty sure I've got one now. I'm under a large canvas, an open-walled tent similar to one I once shared with Mr. Avidità. A soothing breeze caresses me, and it carries the aromas of wildflowers and roasting meat. Without turning my head I know I'm in an encampment—campfire smoke, conversation, the laughter of children. I'm lying in a cot, propped on pillows. Raised on bundles of cloth, my left leg has bled through layers of bandages. At least someone has thrown a sheet over me.

A raven's deep caw draws my attention. Twenty meters from me, Nevermore perches on the lowest branch of an oak tree.

Someone says, "The fool's awake."

A Horned Lord comes into view, standing a few paces beyond the foot of my cot. Two spear-carrying women approach from the right. One holds a simple wooden chair in her free hand, and she sets it beside me.

She's of Japanese descent, I'm certain. Beautiful, difficult to look away from her. Her lips are an unusual mauve, a color I haven't yet seen in the spectra of the Faen, in whatever infects this land.

Backing to the edge of the canvas, she stands guard.

Across camp, Bettina finishes a conversation with two gray-haired men, who bow to her and hurry off on some task. The Queen musses the hair of a young boy, waves to his mother, then crosses the camp. She looks me over and sighs.

"You," she says, "are one dumb sonuvabitch."

I manage a smile. "I like to think of myself as *determined* and *focused.*"

She settles in the chair. "How're you feeling?"

My leg throbs and pain spikes from my knee to my lower back. I try wiggling my toes but can't feel them, can't be sure if they moved or not. My thinking feels fuzzy.

"I'm fine," I say. "I assume I'm on painkillers?"

"Doped out of your mind," she says. "What were you *thinking?* A spy needs to be more than a good observer or a good fighter or a good athlete or a good *swimmer.*"

"What *sort* of painkillers?"

"The strong kind." She sighs. "Foremost a spy needs to be a good liar."

"Yeah?"

Her earthy irises flicker side to side as she studies me. "You're a *terrible* liar."

My laugh is honest and unexpected. "I've got to return to Station."

"That we *cannot* allow you to do, Aur, not yet. You've crossed into the Faen, an unwanted guest."

"Guest?"

"A one-way guest."

"Why?"

"For obvious reasons," she says, "we can't let you report anything you've seen here, not to Avidità, not to anyone else."

"Why not kill me?"

She leans back, resting her hands on her knees. "Don't imagine for a moment your reprieve is permanent, is guaranteed."

"Who determines whether I live or die? You?"

"You, actually." She gestures to a glass water bottle on a wooden table. The Horned Lord brings it to her, and she offers it to me. I hadn't realized how parched I felt, how cracked my lips had become despite the humidity and cold— maybe *because* of the cold and all that time in salt water. "The Faen has you, Aur. *Let* it have you. Everything you once did for Avidità, we want you to do for us."

I guzzle the bottle, and she hands it back to the Horned Lord.

"You want me," I say, "to betray Mr. Avidità? Never to see him again?"

She half shrugs. "Who knows what the future holds? But your only option, Aur, is to say *yes.* "

"If I say *no?* "

Bettina smiles, laying her hand on my shoulder. "The Horned Lord will know if you refuse, or if you lie, as He knew you were lying at Threshold."

I glance at the man standing nearby, a man as shaggy and wild as the other Horned Lords, his antlered headdress touching the tarp above him, his red- and blue-stained leathers marking him as an entity of the forests, no one meant for civilization. His darkly stained lips frown, as all other men like him tend to frown. Yet I *know* Bettina doesn't mean *this* Horned Lord, and it occurs to me *all* the Horned Lords may reflect a single identity, a single expression of *the* Horned Lord, who is no man at all.

The Horned Lord will know if I refuse.

He'll know if I lie.

Uncomfortable, I shift in the cot. "How bad is the leg?"

"Dr. Falwell doesn't know if you'll keep it. Another reason why you won't be returning to San Francisco—or to orbit—anytime soon."

Dr. Jane Falwell, once of Strickland Industries, now a devotee to the Queens.

"Up there," I say, "they could save it."

"Maybe, but you're not 'up there.' Down here the best I'm going to guarantee you is you won't die from gangrene or a Clostridium infection."

"How reassuring."

"Dr. Falwell will check on you this evening," Bettina says, rising from her chair, looking down at me, "assuming you live that long. This afternoon, her nurses will change your bandages."

"When do I receive my sentence?" I ask.

"Sunset." She walks into the daylight, leaning back and closing her eyes to the sky. "You still thirsty, Aur? Hungry?"

"Both. Very."

"The sun is wondrous!" she says. "Would you like to come out and join me?"

Why the hell not? The giggles of children grow louder, some game of chase, as many as a dozen cavorting throughout the forests.

"What's there to eat?" I ask.

She looks over her shoulder, her brown eyes catching the light. "Spring greens, squash, cornbread, rice. Eggs, of course. Baked vegetables. Roasted chicken. Plenty of barbecued rabbit."

"Barbecued rabbit?"

"On these islands there's an overabundance of coney."

"No long pig on offer today?" All those rumors about the Horned Lords and cannibalism.

"On Easter?" Bettina chuckles. "If you need to wash your meal down," she says, "we've got beer and mead too."

"I should stick with water."

"You sure?" she says. "It could be your last day on Earth."

I think she understands the irony.

She also said *barbecued rabbit*.

I'm starving.

EASTER EGGS. Yes, the children were chasing and wrestling and giggling and playing, but they were also hunting for Easter eggs. Scores of eggs around the encampment, dyed brightly and outrageously patterned. In my twenty-seven years I've never participated in an Easter-egg hunt, though I understand quite a few Stations host them, places with Christians.

Here, on Wrangell, this is not a Christian celebration.

Nevermore sometimes circles above us, sometimes flies elsewhere. I seldom notice the moment he comes or goes. Several dozen people of all ages gather here. A fiddler and drummers play ditties which could be centuries old, tunes from the Yukon or Appalachia or Ireland, and listeners dance as they're inspired. At the other side of the clearing, Alastar's nurse holds the infant at her breast. The toddler plays at her feet, a brown-skinned girl with untamed hair.

"She's *your* daughter," I say to Bettina.

"Yes," says the Queen, her gaze wistful, lingering on the children.

"What's her name?"

"Firyali."

A Kenyan word meaning *extraordinary,* if I remember correctly. I feel it wise *not* asking who the father might be. Across the extended encampment, I count a hundred adults. There're dozens of children. I see no easily defined "nuclear" families anywhere.

"What's to happen to Alastar?" I ask.

"What do you mean, 'What's to happen?' We'll raise him as our own."

"I'm happy to hear that."

"Don't misunderstand me," she says, "we know he's *some* trickery of Avidità. I admit, too, I thought he might've been a weapon, suggested killing him the night you arrived."

I don't bother hiding my horror.

"Don't worry," she says. "If Alastar was a *weapon,* Avidità would've used it already, don't you think? There's been ample time."

"I'm sure he's not a weapon," I say.

"Would Avidità have told you if the child *was?*"

I'm not certain.

"The afternoon's getting late," she says. "Sun's almost to the trees. Did you get enough to eat, Aur? Enough to drink?"

"I've had my fill."

From the trees to the east, Cailín and Eagna emerge. The girl holds her puppy, the mottled charcoal fluff ball, which lies contentedly in her arms. Not more than five kilos' worth of dog. I don't figure I'll see the white one but then—

There it is, playing behind her legs.

Eagna looks straight at me, the way she might look at a dull landscape. Stepping behind her mother, she scratches each puppy's head.

"It's time," says Cailín.

Two Horned Lords lift my cot and carry me in the direction from which Cailín arrived. A procession forms, including the Queens, four of their mauve-lipped spearwomen, the Horned Lords, the musicians, Eagna and her puppies, the nurse with Alastar, Firyali, the two gray-haired men, and twenty others. Nevermore caws and croaks and laughs as if at his own private joke.

After a few hundred meters a stand of cedars yields to an expanse of oaks. One in particular towers, its crown overarching the forest, its lowest bows a hundred paces wide. Ribbons of blue and red and purple flutter from its branches.

How can it be that I'm *relieved* to count nine human skulls hanging from its limbs? No vacancies to fill—

On the oak's other side, the circle of white standing stones await us. At their center lies the charred fire pit, and the Horned Lords set me down beside it. The musicians strike a slow rhythm, the fiddler's melody lulling and bittersweet. The gray-haired men hand two folds of cloth to Cailín.

The Queens join me in the circle and the others take up positions outside it. Nevermore disappears into the labyrinth of branches, and the oak darkens, its shadows condensing. Sol settles behind the forests but sponges the western sky in a riot of amber, scarlet, and cobalt.

Bettina sits beside me on the dirt, and she sets a bowl beside her. Cailín circles the pit and, as she does, its fire sparks, grows, and blazes. At its other side she turns toward the oak, raises her arms, and speaks in that strange tongue.

The only word I understand is *Nodens.*

"Listen," I say to Bettina, conscious of the rising panic in my own voice, "I have to tell you something."

She smiles, caresses my cheek, and waits for me to continue. Cailín continues her chant.

"If I don't report back to Mr. Avidità," I say, "he'll finish what he started. He'll destroy you, then he'll destroy the rest of the world." Once the words start coming, they flow. "An ice age! He plans to return the Earth to an ice age. I'm the only one who can stop—"

"Stop," says Bettina, her smile unfaded, her voice gentle. "We already know all that."

Of course they do.

A dusting of aubergine powder coats the bottom of the bowl. Bettina swipes her thumb through it, then pressed her thumb to my forehead, right above my eyes.

No pain this time.

"Tell us," she says, "here in the Grove of the Horned Lord—do you wish to live, or do you wish to die?"

A loss of life, I have always felt, points to some earlier and more essential error and I told myself, before departing EIK-Cel Station, I'd try to get this done without dying. The darkness beneath the oak deepens further, and maybe it's the setting sun or maybe it's something else, but that darkness feels as much like a blanket as it does anything else.

I'll get this done without dying.

"Life," I say. "I choose life."

Bettina's smile is pure cheer, Cailín's words reach a crescendo, and the fire's warmth and light dance with the shadows.

Leaning over me, Bettina slides her hands through my hair. She gazes into my eyes and the tip of her nose brushes mine, a touch easeful and intimate. Lingering in it, she kisses me—

A hint of marshmallow, pepper, and pheromones in the taste of her.

—and she *kisses* me—

—*and she kisses me.*

Horns made of cold flame curl from the sides of her head, encircling her ears. Ewe's horns. The only crown this Queen needs.

Cailín rounds the fire once more, fiery antlers rising above her hair. From the cloths she retrieves two small metallic devices, encased in resin, and she throws these into the fire. I recognize them—Avidità Corporation personal-data trackers.

Bait, now used up.

Again, Bettina kisses me, patient and ambrosial and sovereign. Magic pulses through this land, beacons of Light and rivers of Darkness which appear to me for the first time, spreading from this grove. Wrangell is the center of the cosmos. I vanish into Bettina's kiss and this time I know—

Mr. Avidità and his Corporation.

Nesteler and the UPRC.

All the Gods of the New Moons.

—they haven't got a prayer.

AFTERWORD

I WROTE THIS BOOK'S predecessor in an *epistolary* form, through the journal entries of Bettina Ukweli. Epistolary storytelling is less common in this twenty-first century, but some of the best-known Victorian writers mastered it. *Epistolary* arrives from the Latin *epistolāris,* meaning "that which belongs to a letter." For the Victorians, this included correspondences, contracts, reports, official records, articles, and even journal entries—a letter to oneself. Epistolary stories fascinate me in four ways.

I. Creative Constraints
Epistolary storytelling constrains narrative, even more than limited-third-person or first-person points of view (POVs) do. First- or limited-third-person POVs permit the writer to shift slyly into omniscience. The epistolary POV resists that.

II. Focus
Bram Stoker's *Dracula* is famously epistolary, its narration razor honed. As his characters' story emerged through correspondences, Stoker could waste few words, his exposition confined. Thus, *Dracula's* prose obtains force. By comparison, Stoker's *The Lair of the White Worm* inches along, its prose flaccid, its storytelling limp, its exposition clunky, its characters indistinct.

White Worm employs a mishmash of limited-third person and omniscient third. The epistolary magic which constrained Stoker's worst impulses in *Dracula* appears nowhere in *White Worm.*

III. Unreliable Narrators

Chuck Palahniuk's *Fight Club* gave us one of the most unreliable narrators in all literature. Told in limited first person, *Fight Club* depended upon its narrator's own confusion—and dissociative disorder.

Stories told from multiple first-person accounts generate a similar sense of unreliability. Journals, letters, emails, and communiques of every kind lend themselves to unreliable narration. Competing first-person accounts imply the cracks, inconsistencies, and missing pieces in an incomplete narrative. Who's telling the truth? Who's lying? Who's wrong? Who's right?

Characters, like real people, perceive reality through myriad lenses.

No other storytelling structure creates such tension between narratives as the epistolary. Third person often implies an objectivity; the epistolary makes no such promises.

This is both its strength and its weakness. Some readers, I'm convinced, crave narrative reliability—they want to believe the narrator, or perhaps the writer, is telling the "truth"—but epistolary POVs deny this to both reader *and* writer. The tension this creates is *delicious,* if one can acquire the taste for it.

IV. Voice

Third-person narratives depend upon the singular power of the author's voice. First-person narratives emerge out of a narrower POV, but most first-person stories belong to one character alone—whether in J.D. Salinger's *The Catcher in the Rye* or Jacqueline Carey's *Kushiel's Dart.*

An epistolary story can draw from numerous accounts in many voices. *Dracula's* first hundred pages contain nine unique POVs, told in first and third person. No other form allows an author so many points of view and with so many voices, varying tense, style, language, and grammar.

The *grammar* gives me some consternation. I admit, I worry some readers won't stay with me. For example:

> There, where the UPRC might've killed us, I
> feared for Aurelius more than myself. After all,
> I love him.

That last clause—*I love him*—uses the present tense. As a journal entry, the writer is recounting earlier events, but in writing *I love him,* she's in her mind in the present moment. She still lives, Aurelius still lives, and so her love is in the present too. In a usual third-person narrative, the final clause would have also been in a past tense, as if the entire story occurs in a flash memory on one's deathbed.

In fact, that's how I think of most limited-third-person fiction. This must be one's life, recalled on the deathbed, flashing before one's eyes? Mustn't it?

Yet that is how most authors write most third-person fiction.

Once more, the epistolary gives the writer an immense power of style and voice.

Songs at the End of the World

Each of the *Songs at the End of the World* is at once a first-person account through the eyes of a single character and an epistolary recounting.

Bettina's journal in *When the World Ends.*

In *Gods of the New Moons,* Aurelius lives with a constant narrative, one which he cannot forget. If a Harque survives his mission, he recites his unforgettable narrative, and that narrative becomes part of the official record. Aurelius's ongoing narrative is the mission report not yet written—a field observer's notes, delivered by an observer who needs no notebook.

The next arc of *Songs at the End of the World* will be *Queens of the Horned Lord*. In it we will meet a third narrator who perceives and records her world in still another way.

The fourth, in his own way.

Then finally the fifth.

It is my hope that these novellas will lay the foundations for an even larger work, one whose competing epistolary narratives will weave an interesting song of their own.

In the meantime, I'll continue to work with the very talented musicians at NiceFM, foremost the marvelous Marcus Suraci—aka the Big Makis.

J.L. Forrest

Denver, Colorado
13 February 2019

ABOUT THE AUTHOR

J.L. Forrest has been a college professor, an international scholar, an expatriate, a medal-winning martial artist, a trophy-winning archer, a ticket-winning Skee Ball player, a wilderness survivalist, a sailor, a Fortune 500 consultant, an architect, a horseman, a rock-and-roll guitarist, and an utter layabout. All this amounted to nothing more than preparation for the real challenge—

Writing.

Scrawlings of science fiction and dark fantasy.

Literary musings and whatever else spews from his pen.

He is the award-winning author of dozens of short stories, which have appeared in the likes of *Analog Science Fiction and Fact,* Crossed Genres, Third Flatiron, Robot Cowgirl Press, and others. An active member of the *Science Fiction and Fantasy Writers of America*, J.L. Forrest is also an advocate for literacy, literature, and literary shenanigans of most kinds.

For more than a decade, he has made his primary home in Colorado, but occasionally finds himself ensconced in the Pacific Northwest or in the Old Country of Italia.

In bocca al lupo!

FURTHER READING [AND LISTENING]

Read more of J.L. Forrest—
REQUIES DAWN (a novel of the far future)
DELICATE MINISTRATIONS (short fictions)
MINUSCULE TRUTHS (short fictions)

Songs at the End of the World—
WHEN THE WORLD ENDS
GODS OF THE NEW MOONS
QUEENS OF THE HORNED LORD (Coming 2019)
MEMORIES OF THE DAMNED (Coming 2019)
WHEN THE WORLD BEGINS (Coming 2019)

Join J.L. Forrest's Mailing List—
http://jlforrest.com/newsletter/

Visit J.L. Forrest's Website—
http://jlforrest.com

Listen to the Song for This Novella—
Hear "Re-Entry" by King Makis from NiceFM, and learn more about its creators at:

http://nicefm.bandcamp.com/track/re-entry

IF YOU LIKED THIS story, the best things you can do for the author are **recommend J.L. Forrest's books to others** and **leave a positive review on Amazon**.

www.ingramcontent.com/pod-product-compliance
Lightning Source LLC
Chambersburg PA
CBHW022111170626
46808CB00002B/693